The Physics of Imaginary Objects

Drue Heinz Literature Prize 2010

The Physics of
Imaginary Objects

Tina May Hall

University of Pittsburgh Press

Published by the
University of Pittsburgh Press,
Pittsburgh, Pa., 15260

Manufactured in the United States of America
Printed on acid-free paper
10 9 8 7 6 5 4 3 2 1

Library of Congress Cataloging-in-Publication Data
Hall, Tina May.
  The physics of imaginary objects / Tina May Hall.
  p. cm.
  "Drue Heinz Literature Prize 2010."
  ISBN 978-0-8229-4398-3 (acid-free paper)
  I. Title.
  PS3608.A54824P48 2010
  811'.6 — dc22
                    2010020938

To David and Kristy Hall

Contents

The Physics of Imaginary Objects

Visitations

There was a squirrel trapped in the wall behind my stove in October. We could hear it clawing back there, but what to do? "Maybe it will leave of its own accord," Paul said. We sat at the kitchen table, an old farm table so heavy it took two people to shift it, and listened. Perfect, I thought. One of my friends had come home one night to find her hunter husband had skinned a squirrel and put it in the Crock-Pot. She had lifted the lid expecting rice and beans and had found the pink body curled like a fetus.

One day, I said, "The squirrel's gone—listen, quiet."

He said, "Or it's dead in there."

The stench started three days later. Paul had gone to Phoenix for a conference on new soil technologies, leaving me with the changing leaves and the dead squirrel. At first it was just a tang in the air, sweet-sour, like menstrual blood, like the hair under his arms where I liked to bury my nose. Then it turned gamey, thickened. It spread through the house, a smell that gnawed at me like an itch I could never reach. Paul said it was the baby, said pregnant women had an enhanced sense of smell. Only four months in, and already he had read several books on the subject, was after me to start practicing my breathing and do squats to prepare my pelvic floor. He did not understand it was all I could do to shower and do a little work each day. The morning sickness had not let up, despite what his books predicted. It wasn't really nausea, but more like a shaky hunger, a yearning mixed with claustrophobia. The only thing that helped was meat. Roast beef, steak, sliced ham, chicken cutlets. As long as I ate a good helping of meat every few hours, the sickness stayed at bay, a buzz in my throat. I knew it wasn't really the baby's fault, but I felt robbed of my last few months of freedom. Whenever Paul called from sunny Phoenix, bitterness choked me, made him think I was crying. He was perplexed and irritated. He used words like *miracle* and *new life*. I opened the windows, and the spiders came in. They clustered in the corners of the high ceilings and masqueraded as cracks in the plaster.

October, four years ago, I was also pregnant. This was before Paul. I was a dating a lumberjack who actually wore plaid shirts and had arms like tree trunks and a sweet quirk in his cheek and a habit of cleaning the snow off my truck. When I went to the doctor because my period wouldn't end, she said, "Did you know you were expecting?" I misheard this as expectant and smiled gamely, in a way I thought might be hopeful-looking, wanting to please. Then she took me to a small sterile room and sent me home with a stack of thick cottony maxi-pads like the ones my mother kept in her bathroom cupboard even though she was menopausal. And I was neither mournful nor guilty. It was as if nothing had happened. If I had any feeling about the event, it was a feeling of mild gratitude, the surprise of a small blessing. One night soon after I told him about it, the lumberjack wouldn't come in from chopping firewood. By morning, he had disappeared into the forest, leaving me enough logs stacked against the house to last the winter.

Paul called from Phoenix to tell me about the palm trees. He said they were everywhere, shaggy spires lining the highways and yards. At the conference, they showed pictures of the newest cell phone towers, sculpted to look like everyday objects so that farmers would agree to install them on their land. Everyone liked the one that looked like a windmill. The next time Paul went out, he noticed that some of the palm trees were metal, their split fronds stiff with the business of transmitting and receiving.

When I was alone in the house, something expanded. I slept sprawled across the bed. I left books piled in the living room and plates in the sink. Sometimes it felt like my heart beat so slowly it stuttered and paused, and I could trace the whole path of a leaf falling outside the window before it started again.

The stench kept getting stronger. I could smell it everywhere, even when I was away from the house, walking in the woods, trying to outpace the morning sickness. Even with the cold autumn air stinging my nose, the smell lingered, crouched at the back of my throat, and no amount of swallowing would get rid of it. "We have to do something," I said, the next time Paul called.

He said, "Let's wait it out. It won't last forever."

I met him in a feed store. I was buying tube sand for the back of my truck, and he was checking prices on phosphate. He was a landscape architect starting his own nursery. It was March, and he leaned against the counter, wearing a denim jacket with a dirty sheepskin lining and flirting with the woman ringing up my four bags of tube sand. She must have been eighty years old, and as she ponderously searched out each key on the register and stabbed at it, he said to me, "Isn't a bit late for that?"

He disagreed. He said we met at a wake for a neighbor. I remembered the wake—early spring, the long line of black-clad people strung like beads spilling out of the Victorian house of the mortician—but not him. One of us was forgetting something.

The first snow came while he was still in Phoenix and the dead squirrel was tight in my wall. The small flakes sifted in through the open windows and powdered the hardwood floors. As the snow fell, I felt the baby moving inside me. I hadn't been expecting it for weeks still. Paul had told me that first-time moms often didn't recognize the baby's movements, mistook them for indigestion. It felt like someone tickling me from the inside. I felt bones slipping where there should have been no bones. I went to the stack of pregnancy books on the coffee table and flipped through the pages of the fattest one as if divining from a Bible. My finger stabbed a line drawing of a closed-eyed fetus, its nose tipped up, sniffing, the cord foregrounded, knotted like a sailor's rope. That night, the stars shrank and hardened and the screens in the windows shuddered, punctuating my sleep with aluminum whispers.

My refrigerator was a bloody mess, all that meat rotting imperceptibly. For breakfast, I had half a chicken and I fried a pork chop for a midmorning snack. The baby was hungry for flesh. At the grocery store, I was a werewolf, flinging lamb shanks and ham hocks and rump roasts into the cart. The village ladies giggled and stared at my stomach. The cashier double-bagged everything.

When Paul moved into my house, it was because I refused to spend the night at his. It was a principle of mine to never stay the night at a man's house. And I never had. In all the years of lovers and flings, they always came to me.

I was spending more time in the basement, where the smell was nagging but not unbearable, like a tooth going rotten. The basement was where I had set up my workshop, a grand name for a couple of banquet tables and old file cabinets filled with paints. The knives I kept in a rack on the wall. The handles were black with touch, but the blades shone, oily and flexible. I used linoleum blocks for my woodcuts, and in the cold weather I wrapped them in a heating pad to rid them of their stiffness. Magazines bought these illustrations more often than one might think—duck hunting at dawn, lost in the woods, the persistent mayfly, bear attack.

One morning, soon after the first snow, a bird tried to get into the house. I was coming upstairs from the basement, and the full stench of the squirrel hit me before I heard the thumps. For a moment, my heart jumped—I thought the squirrel had come alive and was trying to escape. Then I went into the kitchen where the smell was most dense and I saw the bird, a small brownish-gray one, maybe a sparrow or a wren, hurling itself at the window. Finally, it stopped, and I went outside to look for its body, but nothing was there, just a few feathers on the ground and a tear in the screen.

The story of the bird didn't seem to upset Paul. He said it was the change of seasons and he'd seen it happen before. He said Phoenix was still hot and fragrant with bougainvillea and chives. He said the woman who ran the bed-and-breakfast had a wonderful yard filled with stones and cacti and tropical blossoms. I asked when he was coming home. The conference was over, but he was learning about conifers and water conservation from a soil engineer he had met there. I reminded him winter was coming.

Paul had moved in during the summer, and the first thing he did was plant a ribbon of hyssop that smelled of licorice and drew the bees. Next, he planted a vegetable garden in the backyard, at the edge of the forest. He said it was too late to plant anything but kale and radishes—bitter, earthy things. When he found out I was pregnant, he was angry I wouldn't marry him. He was angry it took me three weeks to tell him and that when I did, I said I was considering my options. From the garden at his own house, which was only two miles away straight through the woods, he brought tomatoes and yellow squash and peas, which he shelled on the porch while I worked downstairs. All things I couldn't bear to eat. I gnawed at bones while he made summer soups and pastas. I could see his feet moving past the high windows at the top of the basement as he dug dozens of holes around the house—"Surprises," he said, when I asked him about it, things that wouldn't come up until spring.

Wasps came in through the torn kitchen screen. They made their way to the basement and buzzed me as I worked. They were building a nest in the corner of the room, above the water

Every now and again, I tested my limits. I went for hours without eating until the sickness was so bad that I could hardly move for the shaking. Then there would be that scrabbling feeling, that little bony body twisting inside me. On the ultrasound, its spine had been a line of seeds, its fingers twigs finer than anything I could have cut.

The radio in the truck ran reports of home invasions, terrorist alerts, deadly viruses—all stories of hospitality abused. The wasps continued to seep into the basement, and the deer showed up each night to scrape at the door. It began to seem there was something gone wrong in the house. I had spent several winters there, and the animals never had acted like this. I couldn't help but wonder if Paul had brought something with him, a ghost or a curse or an unhappy soul. I went through the two cardboard boxes of clothes he was still living out of and found nothing unusual except for a sock of mine. It was from my favorite pair—a fuzzy lurid pink sock with a cartoonish Virgin Mary stitched in blue. I couldn't tell if the sock had dropped into his box by accident or if he had taken it for some reason, maybe to stop me from wearing them around the house all the time, maybe for love. I left it there, tucked into the sleeve of one of his shirts.

The walls in my house were poorly plastered, the joints in the sheets of drywall rising up like veins in the back of a hand. I considered knocking a hole in the kitchen wall myself and entered the kitchen with an old silk scarf tied around my face. The scarf had been my mother's and smelled like one of her drawers of clothing, dust and lemons. In the kitchen, all I could smell was the squirrel. I leaned against the heavy, old, cast-iron stove but couldn't heater, and I didn't bother them because I hoped it might be one of those large paper nests so prized by artists and naturalists that one sometimes found for sale in junk stores. I would have liked to see how such an elaborate home evolved, but it quickly became clear they were just regular wasps building a mud nest. I ventured into the kitchen for the fruit that was rotting on the counter and piled it on my worktable. The two plums and a soft, late-season tomato lured the wasps, and they posed for me, busy and unhurried, as I cut them into the linoleum blocks. I sent those prints to a women's magazine for a story about love betrayed.

Ten days after the squirrel died in my wall, the smell moved into the bedroom, and I gathered up the down comforter and the Mexican blankets and started sleeping in my pickup truck. The mornings were cold enough that when I woke, the windows were misted with frost and the rough fiberglass ceiling of the camper dripped condensation.

One night, while sitting in the back of the truck, bundled in covers that held the faint scent of the squirrel, I argued with Paul and heard my voice echo back through the cell phone, dummy windmills and palm trees working overtime in the expanse of country between us. As I hung up, a large, dark shape moved past the truck toward the house. There were three deer there, sniffing at the kitchen door. One of them butted its head against the wood. The smell of the squirrel rose up around me like the scent of one's own scalp or the hidden folds of one's skin. The deer made odd sounds, muted moans and snuffles, and tapped their noses against the door as if demanding to be let in.

budge it. The woman I bought the house from had told me the stove used to sit away from the wall to leave space for a box where she slept as a child through the northern winters. A dangerous practice, I had thought at the time.

At night, the baby was particularly active, twisting and squirming inside me. If I spoke or sang, it stilled. I liked it for its caution. I always piled the blankets highest around my middle, even if it meant my feet grew chilled. I sang colors to counteract the onset of gray winter. Cadmium yellow, brown madder, cerulean blue, I whispered, invoking pause.

It snowed again, and I shut the windows to prevent water damage to the wood floors. There was nothing to do but to call the contractor in town. He said he'd send his cousin who had come down from Canada to work through the winter. His cousin was an artist, he said, a master of restoration, and I explained I just needed a hole, an extraction, and a patch, nothing fancy. Really, I just needed someone to help me move the heavy parts of my house, but I didn't want to admit that Paul was still in Phoenix, under the spell of succulents and irrigation systems.

The cousin was older than I had expected, in his late thirties, and I wondered what kind of life he had in Canada that he could leave behind for months at a time. He went unerringly to the wall in the kitchen and stood looking at it, still in his coat and leather work gloves. I apologized for the heat being off and gestured at the wall, the smell, in explanation. Together, we moved the heavy stove and he took off his gloves, placed them carefully in the pockets of his coat, and kneeled to put his bare hand on the plaster. He said he'd have to leave the wall open for a while to air it out, but that he would come back and patch it so perfectly that no one would guess it had ever been touched. I looked at the snowflakes melting in his hair and without knowing why, placed my own hand at the back of his neck, just at the point where his hair met the corduroy collar.

The kitchen table was just as hard and uneven as I had thought it would be, and I worried about splinters, even while enjoying the warmth of him against my ribcage and thighs. He was slow and silent and didn't seem to notice the solid bulge of my belly. *A minor restoration*, I thought as I breathed against his stubbly throat. My fingers measured the ridges of his collar as he moved over me. From that angle, I could see how the aged glass of the windows was much thicker at the bottom than the top, and it seemed for a moment that I could see it slide downward, cloudy, viscous, sinking under its own weight.

When the contractor's cousin finished cutting the hole in the wall, he called to me to come see what he had found. Instead of one squirrel, there were twenty or so, twined around each other, decaying into one mass. They had obviously followed each other down into the space and had not been able to find their way back out.

While he cleared away the bodies in the kitchen, I stayed in the basement. Though I hadn't eaten yet that day, my stomach was calm. I remembered the leaking mass of squirrel upstairs. Nothing. I thought of zucchinis and tomatoes. Nothing. I imagined eating eggplant, asparagus, endive with sliced radishes. The baby squirmed a little but that was all. The sickness seemed to have disappeared, just as the books said, with no warning. My whole body, even my skin, relaxed, no longer braced against the nausea. The contractor's cousin's boots tapped on the floor above me, making trips from wall to door. I made a woodcut of a charmed house, surrounded by birds and deer and squirrels and wasps. I was working on a buck rearing upright when he called down to me that he was finished, and the knife slipped, gouging away one of the deer's legs before sliding into the thumb of my left hand. When I went upstairs to pay him, he looked at my hand wrapped in the scrap of an old t-shirt starting to seep blood, but he didn't say anything until I handed him the money, and then he said, "Thank you"—twice he said it, shyly, not meeting my eyes.

Paul called to say he was coming home. I was in the basement working on a print for a nature magazine of a man in a forest holding up an old-style lantern—lost in the snow. I struggled with the flakes falling through the tree branches—a tricky thing, determining how much to pare away. My cut thumb stung, reminded me to go slowly.

When Paul walked into the kitchen, he gasped at the hole in the wall and the smell that lingered. It was clear we were not going to be able to stay in the house. He stood in the center of the room, looking around, and I saw him touch the table, noticing it was shifted from its usual space.

There was no use in taking anything with us because the smell had permeated everything. His house was only a few miles through the woods, and we decided to celebrate the first real snowfall by snowshoeing there. It was already night. The air was so cold the trees cracked. Above us, the gibbous moon, deflating. Between us, this understanding, a tether, the thing we wouldn't talk about. I wanted to tell him about the kitchen windows, the thickness of glass, the cost of a wall filled with squirrels, the spiders claiming their corners. I wanted to tell him I loved him and I couldn't remember how we met. He had things he wanted to tell me too; I knew by the way his breath hung in the air before us. There were so many things inside us, and it comforted me to think of them there, curled up, content, for the time being, to be hidden.

Erratum:
Insert "R" in "Transgressors"

Fragments from the 1899 and 1900 *Transactions of the American Microscopical Society*

A murder had been committed, the instrument used being an ax.

The victim was a sailor of Swedish extraction and had sailed the lakes for seven or eight years, making his home in Buffalo.

The defendant was a dancer, a singer, a woman once beautiful who, because of her tortuous course, became roughened and changed.

The victim was a sailor of Swedish extraction. He was in the habit of spending his nights when on shore at a notorious dance hall in the infected district.

I was engaged as a medical expert in an investigation under peculiar circumstances. With your kind permission, I will briefly narrate.

The poetic statement that drops of different bloods drying on a glass plate would give different figures needs only to be mentioned to show that science is not always divorced from fancy.

The victim was a sailor of Swedish extraction. He was in the habit of spending his nights in the infected district. One night he met a singer, whose husband was "the strong man" doing certain tricks such as stone-breaking, tearing chains asunder, and the like. One night the sailor met a singer, a woman, once beautiful, whose very appearance struck him a blow.

A murder had been committed, the instrument used being an ax. After the murder, the house, a wooden one, containing the body, was set on fire, burning to the ground.

I was engaged as a trained and thorough observer, called into action to help solve the seeming mystery. I was engaged for the testimony of a microscopist—one who sees, then feels—not with his fingers but with his intellectual grasp. With your kind permission, I will briefly narrate.

A murder had been committed, the instrument used being an ax. After the murder, the house, a wooden one, containing the body, was set on fire, burning to the ground. The ax had been thrown down about eight feet from the house, thus being subjected to a high heat.

I was engaged to determine the presence or absence of blood.

The defendant was a woman, a singer in a resort, whose husband was "the strong man" doing certain tricks. Her very appearance struck the sailor a blow. The sailor's was a stable body not readily affected. He was of Swedish extraction. He had sailed the lakes for seven or eight years.

The victim may have been the husband, "the strong man" noted for his strength, which in fact consisted only in stage tricks. One man was missing, one dead.

A trauma, be it ever so slight, is only safe as long as the pressure is low. A glance from her struck the sailor a blow. The action of the heart alone is almost never responsible. She was a singer in the infected district, which caused her to become roughened and changed.

I was engaged as a medical expert, a trained and thorough observer, called into action to help solve a seeming mystery.

One man was missing, one dead. They offer a point of least resistance, and upon the degree of resistance do their own lives and safety depend.

To determine the presence or absence of blood, one must perform the most delicate test. The action of the heart alone is almost never responsible.

A glance from her struck him a blow. One man was missing, one dead. Her husband was "the strong man" doing certain tricks, such as stone breaking, tearing chains asunder, and the like.

A chain is no stronger than its weakest link, or a bridge stronger than its weakest span, or a man stronger than his weakest artery.

He was a sailor of Swedish extraction who was in the habit of spending his nights in the infected district. There he met women who were usually functional and temporary. She was a singer, once beautiful. They proceeded upstairs to a private room. A glance from her struck him a blow.

A bridge is no stronger than its weakest span. There can be no question about the delicacy of this reaction. The main force of the heart is spent in distending the arteries. A man is no stronger than his weakest artery. They offer a point of least resistance, and upon the degree of resistance does their own life and safety depend.

Leaving the room and descending the stairs, they met the husband who struck the sailor on the jaw, felling him. One man was missing, one dead. The house, a wooden one, was set on fire, burning to the ground. A murder had been committed, the instrument used being an ax. On the ax were charred and brittle hairs and some brownish-black spots, which, if blood, were too much altered to respond to any but the most delicate test.

I was engaged as a trained observer—one who sees, then feels—not with his fingers but with his intellectual grasp. As a stable body not readily affected. As a microscopist and a medical expert. With your kind permission, I will briefly narrate.

Practically everything can be accomplished with the small direct vision.

One man was missing, one dead. The woman was a singer, once beautiful, capable of striking a blow with a glance. The instrument used being an ax. Her husband was "the strong man," noted for his strength, which in fact consisted only in stage tricks. He struck the sailor on the jaw, felling him. On the ax were brownish-black spots. The test is certain and quite delicate. The sailor was of Swedish extraction and had sailed the lakes. A bridge is no stronger than its weakest span.

Only the use of the most exact and accurate appliances could lead to successful or trustworthy conclusions. They proceeded upstairs to a private room. The main force of the heart is spent. A murder had been committed. To withstand the force of the heart's action one becomes roughened and changed. Matters of the most vital concern may be at stake, with a single small fragment at hand for examination.

There is yet no accord. How to withstand the force of the heart's action? The test is certain and quite delicate. A bridge is no stronger than its weakest span. How to withstand the force of the heart's action? I was engaged as a trained and thorough observer. The main force of the heart is spent. The vessel walls will yield to the strain. The instrument used being an ax. How to withstand the force of the heart's action? Only the use of the most exact and accurate appliances. Practically everything can be accomplished with the small direct vision. How to withstand the force of the heart's action? A murder, an ax, drops of different bloods, a blow, stage tricks, the tearing asunder of chains, the house, a wooden one, burned to the ground, the heart, the infected district.

Skinny Girls' Constitution and Bylaws

We will know each other by the way our watches slip from our wrists, the bruises on our knees, our winged shoulder blades tenting silk dresses.

We eat; we eat. We eat like wild boars, like wolves, like cyclists in training. We love the bloody shreds that cling to the T. We suck the gob of marrow that floats to the top of the soup. We gnaw the chicken down to splinters.

Everything is bone, bone, bone.

Her brother holds Polly to the candle to read her, the way one would a stolen envelope. Numbers float like seaweed under her skin. She is a mathematical genius. She has teeth like the keys of an adding machine. She tells her brother that his birth date plus his wedding date plus the date of his death add up to 243. He drops her so quickly the flame is blown out.

They call us witches. They look away from us in the bright light. The lavender crisps in the fields. The rain will not come.

Querida is the only one of us who once was fat. Her mother cooked with lard and made pink pastries on the weekends. But when she was thirteen, Querida got her period and a fever in the same week. She burned and burned. The priests said masses over her. Her bed was lit by a hundred candles. Her mother held a wet cloth to her brow for fifteen months while bees died in the space between the window and screen. And when she rose up, Querida was a blade of grass, sweet as spit, forehead blanched and thighs withered. We ask her what it was like and pinch her waist, but she only smiles. We love our secrets; anything hidden is so dear to us, we who are always on display.

When we run, our knees are castanets.

Thirteen of us, a baker's dozen. Pasteboard box of meringues, sweet and brittle. Thirteen horses wheeling at the fence. Thirteen water-striders, all legs and surface tension.

Bianca's job is to fasten ties around men's necks all day long. She has mastered the Windsor, the half-Windsor and the four-in-hand. She is practicing the cross knot. The double-simple is best for short men. Only a few wear bowties. Most prefer silk to polyester. Cotton is a daring choice. Bianca's fingers move quick as crickets. Many of her clients don't even realize she is there. The worst part is the collars. They are always too narrow or wide, too dingy or floppy. Bianca takes home the collars of the men she likes best and stiffens them herself with sugar and egg whites and mineral water, boiled down to a paste, painted on with a dove's feather, dried by her own breath.

We will gestate plump happy babies in the bone cages of our pelvises.

When we lift our arms to the moon, there is a sound like branches scraping.

Lizzie stops a car with her bare hand, standing in the middle of the road over the body of the dead fox. The car just kisses the skin of her palm as it drifts to rest, like a boat easing into dock. Beneath the wishbone of her legs, the fox shudders. The moon falls right out of the sky. Fur springs up to cover wounds, its tail traces an "S" on the asphalt.

We chant Plath at school assemblies. "One year in every ten, peel off the napkin, I eat men, I eat men," as we shake our pom poms and swivel our hips, left, right, all around, a racetrack, a snake eating its tail, the eternal omphalos. Our classmates love it, throw carnations at us, send us candy-grams and risqué text messages, dream of us all weekend long.

We will donate cells drawn from the doorknobs of our spines, the needle a key turning us.

At eight, Francie is the youngest of us. We feed her the choicest bits, the organ meats and the toenails, the nose cartilage. She is pretty as a stream, kind as a blizzard, graceful as a schooner a thousand feet underwater. She plays goalie on the hockey team and roars like a lion when she has a bad dream. She will not sleep alone; her fears are our fears. Her knuckles dig into our necks at night; her mouth touches ours when we least expect it. Little ghost, how often we have closed the door on you, how often you have tunneled through.

We will not stick our heads in ovens. We will not throw ourselves from bridges, nor weight our pockets, nor disturb our veins.

Nessa is the mean one, the one who deals with telemarketers and credit card bills. She never holds the door for anyone, puts the empty milk carton back in the fridge, tells people their pets are ugly and ill-behaved. In her spare time, she climbs, her feet wedged into the too-small shoes, her fingers caked with chalk. Once, she fell sixty feet and dangled there, hanging from the rope and a leaf-bladed piton, the last of three, the only one to hold. She broke all of her fingers that time, trying to find a way up or down. In the end, she swears she used her teeth to unclip the carabiners and release herself from the granite face into the air, where she floated, hollow as a feather, lightning cracking around her, knowing what was coming, the morphine and its weird itch, the feeling of her tibia stitching itself back together, the forever lumpiness of her ribs, the first drops of rain, heavy as lead on her skin.

We will grow up to be doctors and stockbrokers and video store clerks. We will wear our hair like crowns and snort through flared nostrils.

Martine is 115 years old and still flat-chested. In her cold, blue heart, three little men live. By night, they write love poems and keep her awake with their sighing. By day, they smoke cigarettes and discuss Nietzsche. Finally, they lick clean the last can of duck fat, cough up their black lungs, and wither into tiny skeletons, whose splintery outlines Martine can feel if she presses hard enough.

We pass each other notes in the hollows of our collarbones.

In the snow, Audrey is invisible. Her pink cheeks drain to white, her eyes pale, her skin turns waxy. She is the corpse-bride running after the soccer ball. She is the one who chirps, "We're late again," hands around lunches in paper bags, and builds scale replicas of Chartres out of the ice she scrapes from the windshield. Inside, Audrey is always the first to be seen. She is all roses and oranges and zebra stripes. She jingles when she walks — it is her molars rattling.

There is no noose that can hold us.

Fiona writes romance novels on her cell phone during lunch hour. All of her heroines are named Fiona, and her heroes are prone to swooning. Her publisher pays her in pounds and thinks she is a little old grandmother in County Cork. She writes, "Mark clapped the back of his hand to his forehead and said, 'I am overcome.'" And, "Frank sank gracefully onto the divan." And, "Steve reached out blindly as the world went gray."

Underwater, we are transparent.

Our mothers won't let us sit on their laps.

Colleen is deaf. We broke all of our grandmothers' rose-decaled plates proving it. We speak to her in signs and spell out the unusual words. *Filament, Frangipani, Balzac.* She sings us to sleep with her stony voice. She wakes at dawn to bake saffron buns with fat raisins poking out like roaches. In public, we must be careful. The sight of our fingers spelling causes heart attacks and car accidents. Mostly, we wait to talk in the dark, in bathroom stalls and movie theaters, broom closets and basements, our hands pressed into her hand, our knuckles kissing.

We fit six across the backseat and shiver together, arms and legs wrapped like eels around each other.

Olivia, Ophelia, and Odette are identical triplets. They have red hair that has never been cut. They sleep on piles of it, bind it up in knots and rolls for the daytime, let it unfurl like bolts of silk after dark. They sing in unison, their clear voices making a chord. They tap dance and juggle knives. They do a ventriloquist act at the burlesque theater downtown. Between the strippers, the triplets appear, holding three dolls with long, red hair. They are perfectly synchronized; they never falter. Their lips don't move. Once in a while, a chartreuse feather floats down from the catwalk or the light shifts and the stage glitters with loosened sequins. For the finale, they sit perfectly still, until the audience forgets which are the dolls and which the girls and breaks into spontaneous applause.

We will grow up to be spelunkers, ballerinas, and landscape architects.

In fairy tales, we are the last to be eaten.

They call us late bloomers, daddy longlegs, frigid. They call us by each other's names and names we've never known and seat us in the back row of the plane, not realizing that it is our prayers keeping everyone from going down in a scream of burning metal. They call us *sweetheart* in the dark, never guessing we are all around them, so many of us packed in tight. That old game, we think. Breast, hip, thigh. *Sardines*, it was called, and the goal was to stay hidden.

We wash in teacups. We chart the stars on our scapulae, make telescopes of thumbs and forefingers. We cut our nails short as boys', the better to scratch at the chiggers embedded in our shins. We know our blood is sweet to drink; we know our bones are irresistible.

Kick

Last night, Ben dreamed of Freud and woke up laughing. He remembered this suddenly, as the lawn chair with its frayed, vinyl strips creaked against his fidgeting. Pale Johnnie threw two more steaks on the grill and some sausages and a bouquet of tender, pink chicken breasts. This was the monthly distance-running club gathering, and they were all on high-protein diets. Ben ran the farthest of them all, though Marco was the fastest. Ben was also the oldest of them, by nine years, an eternity to a runner, nearly two age groups. He shifted again, folding and unfolding his grasshopper legs.

Across the field, Jessamy was playing with the kids, throwing a kite into the air, trying in vain to catch a scrap of breeze. It was July, and the air was like honey. She called to the little boy holding the string (one of Pale Johnnie's kids—hair the same brush of white blond), "Run, run." And the boy ran, dragging the kite behind him, the tip tripping over the stubbly earth. Jessamy was a runner too but only marathons, not ultramarathons, and she walked through the water stops. At Ben's events she took photos, shuttling from point to point to catch him. Invariably in these photos, Ben was mid-stride, mouth agape, left shoulder higher than the other, hands clenched. The other members of the club looked at the photos and chided him for the tense posture, talked about minutes he could shave off if he would relax his upper body. That was one of the highlights of these gatherings, race photo analysis. Along with talk of tapering strategies and shoe inserts and the best podiatrists in the area, the ones who would shoot you up with cortisone and not explicitly tell you to stay off your feet. Sometimes, when one of Ben's runs was over rough terrain, Jessamy brought her bike and she would buzz up to him out of the woods, spewing cedar chips and flecks of mud, snap her photos, and spin away. Ben thought of her as some kind of wood sprite in those moments, a distraction, a glimpse of color and a whir of wings. Jessamy was certainly sprite-like. Anyone would agree. Had there been a strong wind, the kite could have lifted her off of her feet. Ben thought of it, Jessamy, floating overhead, her blue sundress ballooning around her skinny legs, her sandals slipping off one by one to fall into the duck pond.

Jessamy wanted children, and Ben didn't. He didn't like the way they drooled and clung and had to be carried everywhere. That morning, after he had woken up laughing, Ben had gone to his lab and euthanized forty-two rove beetles to send to a fifth-grade class in Florida. When he had put them all in the killing jar along with the tablespoon of nail polish remover, all forty-two opened their mandibles at him and waved their abdomens threateningly. This was the type of moment that made Ben love being an entomologist, even though his running buddies introduced him as "the bug man" and he knew they found his job somehow ridiculous. As a boy, Ben had been happiest when he was lying outside at night, the air buzzing and crawling around him, his hands wrapped around one of the glass mason jars his grandmother saved for him. Jessamy wanted a dog, and Ben didn't. He didn't like the way they drooled and shed and had to be taken outside to shit. Jessamy wanted a velour couch and an inflatable travel bed and the color green on the kitchen walls. Jessamy wanted a lot of things Ben didn't. That morning he had labeled the box going to Florida in his flowery script and written underneath *rove beetle, Staphylinus olens*, and under that, *often called the Devil's Coach Horse*. On impulse, he drew a picture of the beetle on the side of the box, meticulously inked and shadowed, the kind of illustration he normally was paid quite a bit of money to produce.

Pale Johnnie had a nice spread. It was one of those farms that no longer functioned as such and instead was just a big, nostalgic playground for parents and children. The fields lay fallow and the barn housed a jumble of tricycles and beach floats, plastic balls and dolls, and hoops and teepees—everything inflatable. Pale Johnnie was going on about the trees in the field, how he had some agreement with the government not to let them grow and now the seedlings, too large to tug out, had to be poisoned, one by one, with some liquid so toxic that Pale Johnnie administered it with an eyedropper. A small, plastic hatchet was wedged into a stump by the barbeque grill; a decaying Day-Glo orange semiautomatic water gun lay near Ben's feet. He prodded at it with a toe, but it seemed rooted to the ground.

If Jessamy flew away, Ben would be sad but also very happy, relieved even. Sometimes he imagined ways she might die on her way home from her job at the daycare center and reassured himself that every married person did this now and again. His favorite was collision with an oil tanker because the body would be incinerated, leaving fewer details for him to fuss with in the midst of his bereavement. If Jessamy flew away, Ben would eat all of the casseroles that were stacked in the freezer, and surely there would be a stream of additional casseroles brought by neighbor ladies.

"Did you know you are harboring bald-faced hornets?" Ben called to Pale Johnnie, gesturing to the nest hanging from the barn eaves.

Marco's girlfriend, who was curled up on a beach towel next to Marco's chair, said, "Are they the ones always missing a leg?" She was big-bosomed and wore enormous, magenta-tinted sunglasses that matched her fingernail polish. She appeared to be nameless and, like all of Marco's girlfriends, seemed not to notice that he was just using her for sex. Ben had no idea what she was talking about. "You know," she said earnestly. "They are on my screens all the time, big ugly suckers with claw legs, all lop-sided like."

Ben said, "That doesn't sound like a wasp at all."

Any rational man would lust after Marco's girlfriend, but Ben was drawn instead to Pale Johnnie's wife who, as far as he knew, had never painted her nails in her life. She also did not run but stayed at home baking zucchini bread and watching the kids while Pale Johnnie took to the road nearly every weekend for the race season from April to October. They had four boys, all loud and blond. Meg had large hips and wore khaki shorts that were perpetually wrinkled in unflattering ways. She sat with her thighs apart and her head cast back, snoring slightly in the chair next to Ben. The youngest son, still a baby really, was snuggled into her belly, his face nuzzled into her shirt. Ben imagined the folds of her skin were crusted with spit-up and potato salad, that she was the kind of woman with a disintegrating Kleenex tucked into her bra. Her hair frizzed everywhere and her arms were freckled like a giraffe's skin. She had beautiful knees, perfectly round and aligned, no scars or arthroscopic puckers. They were the knees of a woman half her age. Ben wanted to take one in each hand and just hold it, like an apple. He felt aroused just thinking of it, picturing himself kneeling between her legs, cupping each precious knee.

The sun was setting, and a breeze finally kicked up. Ben heard Jessamy's squeal of excitement. The chicken charred on the grill. In the barn, five hundred wasps hatched in unison. Ben flexed his Achilles tendon compulsively, absentmindedly, like a violinist tapping out a rhythm with his toes. Across the field of dead and unplanned plants, the kite ripped into the air.

For Dear Pearl, Who Drowned

She wakes thinking today she'd like to eat eggs. All night she dreamed of a hard-boiled one, white and gold. She wakes thinking an egg is something beautiful to own. The sun is bright in the shelter. All the windows are bare. The sun is as bright as a memory. The sun is too bright in her. It is as bright as

Her knees glow in the shower. She scrubs them hard. They are red and wistful. She has given up on soap. Soap is for sisters taking baths together. Soap tastes like Sunday nights. Now, everything is scrubbing. She scrubs too hard to be clean. It is hard to scrub oneself clean. It is hard to be clean. It is hard to be

The man who stands next to the doughnut shop is dirty. He has long hair like vines. He asks her questions. His hair twists words. His hair spells starvation. She pays for a piece of it. She pays for a piece of hair to make a rope of. She pays for a piece of hair to weave a meal of. It is hard. It is hard to make anything clean.

Her knees hurt too much to walk outside in the sunlight. The sun can hurt. Sometimes a child is at school during a solar eclipse. Sometimes a child is at recess during a solar eclipse. Sometimes a child is waiting for her turn on the swingset when everything is shadow.

She remembers. She remembers that one can go blind and not even know it. She remembers the sun isn't always bright. The sun can make things dark. She remembers how the sun can make everything

Inside the drugstore there is shade. Everything is hidden from the sun. She is hiding enough hair for a meal. There is a storekeeper to hide from. But he is watching television. He does not see her. He can see paper-thin people. He has mirrors to watch them. He has a television. He has a special type of vision because his store is so dark. But he does not see her. He doesn't want to. He has a television instead of the sun. He has a television to make things bright. He has a way of making people paper-thin.

A lot of things can feed a person. It doesn't have to be a snare made of hair. She loosens pills from their boxes and bottles to see them. She doesn't like the brown pills. She doesn't like the red pills, either. Brown and red are colors for leaves in the forest. Brown and red can be stretched into squares on a pretend sofa. Brown and red leaves are big enough to block the sun. Brown and red leaves are big enough for paper dolls to live in. But not big enough for her.

Paper dolls never die. But their heads fall off. Sometimes sisters play on brown and red leaves with paper dolls. They have to be careful. Even when wrapped with Scotch tape the necks are too fragile.

The storekeeper's mouth opens wide when he laughs. But then it closes again. She saw, though. She saw silver hidden in his teeth. She saw silver like stars. He laughs again. The people on the television are so paper-thin it's funny. The people on television are so thin you can see through them. They would not make a good eclipse. She finds the white pills.

These are the ones she likes.

These are the ones smooth enough to be eggs. Eggs can only grow smooth in the water. Eggs only grow smooth with a lot of scrubbing. These are the ones smooth enough to be her knee-caps. She scrubs her body every morning as if

It's hard to make a clean meal. But it is easier if the pills are white. The pills have to be white and stolen. The pills have to be white as the sun. The pills have to be white as soap on Sunday. She hides them in her shoes. The storekeeper is laughing, not laughing. Each time he opens his mouth, the store gets darker.

She has to go back into the sun. But she walks close to the buildings to avoid noon. Her kneecaps don't like day. Neither do her elbows. Day means sun. Day means a knob in the shower that has to be turned all the way. Day means hot. It has to be hot enough to

Her kneecaps and her elbows like shadows. They like wrinkles. They treasure most skin that has pulled away from the sun. Every morning she scrubs away the wrinkles. Her elbows cry all day for more.

They were proud of that skin.

She walks close to the buildings to hide from sun. She is searching for something to eat. She is searching for food, maybe the kind of food that comes from a door marked *Palm Reader*. The kind of meal that can read wrinkles in a hand. The kind that maps lines in skin. Wrinkles can be translated into words. Wrinkles are dangerous. She tries to scrub them smooth as eggshell. She tries to wear them down. But her skin resists her. Her skin resists water. Her skin is too proud.

The palm reader tells her to put her hand on the table. She tells her to put two dollars on the table.

The palm reader is a large woman with no hair. She has teeth even and white like a painting. She has teeth like a photograph in a magazine, like a row of quail eggs. They don't look real.

The palm reader is touching her hand, testing the thickness of skin. She says it's not worth telling futures, only pasts. The palm reader touches her hand. She watches her skin stretch. Her skin is trying. Her skin is trying to give up a memory. It is hard to remember. She scrubs every morning to forget. It is hard to be clean. It is hard to remember without wrinkles.

The palm reader says *river*. A river is a way to eat. A way to wait for the fat ones to drink, to step into the trap. And if that doesn't work, there are fish with their spider bones and their slipshine eyes like coins in a pocket.

Sometimes a sister dies in a river.

Sometimes two sisters are playing and one goes into the river. Sometimes two sisters are playing tea party with white cups and imaginary boiled eggs and brown and red leaves by the water when everything is shadow.

A river is not a clean death.

Sometimes a sister looks at the sun so long she goes blind for a little bit. Sometimes when she can see again, something is missing. A river is not clean. There is no way to look through it, to see what might be hiding inside. Sometimes the skin resists water. Sometimes a person stays in the bath too long. Sometimes a person stays in water long enough to grow wrinkles. Sometimes a person stays in water even longer. She says *river*. The palm reader's room is shaking. The palm reader's earrings are trembling. Everything is falling. She sees an eclipse. She feels an earthquake. She sees an eclipse moving over the lamp. It is only a cat.

The palm reader tells her how to find an egg. She tells her to go out the back door and to make a cup with her mouth. The palm reader tells her to walk until she finds running water. Her hand is still on the table. Her skin is listening. Her skin knows about water. Her skin knows about scrubbing. Her skin knows how to

It is hard to make a clean meal. She finds a back door. She walks for a long time. She walks for a long time but doesn't find water. She only finds a highway. Sometimes a highway can be a river. Sometimes a cat can be an eclipse. She hangs her feet in the water. She hangs her feet in the water to search for smooth stones. The water is too dirty to see through. She has to search by touch.

She remembers the piece of hair and makes a line of it. She remembers the pills and makes bobbers of them. A newspaper man on the median is busy selling disaster. He gives her a lump of grief that has hardened at the bottom of the canvas pocket at his waist. He gives her a hard lump of grief to use as bait. It rings like a coin in the river. She makes a cup with her mouth.

She hangs her feet in the water to feel the stones rolling. She hangs her feet in the water to search by touch. She sees silver. She sees silver spinning down the river. She sees silver like stars. She sees the lures that other people cast. She sees a lot of silver. It is hard to catch anything clean. The river is polluted now. It is dangerous to eat from it.

The river hides things in its wrinkles. She pulls the piece of hair in and throws it back out. She pulls the piece of hair in to check her bait. She pulls the piece of hair in and sees a hard lump of grief. It is a hard enough lump to last for a while. It is hard enough to last for a while even in water.

The sun goes away. Her kneecaps forget to be quiet and sigh at the darkness. Her kneecaps sigh at not having to hide anymore. Her kneecaps count their wrinkles. The only light is from stars. She sees stars streaming by her. She sees stars like silver. She sees stars like teeth, like teacups, like eggs. She sits still, and the stars move and flash around her.

They don't spell anything. They don't remember anything.

She makes a cup of her mouth and the egg flesh fills it. She bites down hard and the yolk breaks. A million lovely yellow pieces of yolk melt onto her tongue. Eating an egg is like dying — it is so beautiful, all on its own, without any help. The egg in her mouth is a blessing of flesh and salt and yellow. The eggs under her feet roll like stones. The egg in her hand is as pure as the heart of a sister, white and hard, strong egg, like a star, like a pearl, grown up around its powdery secret.

Faith Is Three Parts Formaldehyde,
One Part Ethyl Alcohol

Rosa keeps her finger in a jar on the nightstand. In the morning, it twists to feel the sunlight. She watches its gentle convulsions and holds her other fingers up to share the warmth. Since she cut off her finger, she has worked in the diocese business office, filing and answering phones. Mostly, she answers questions from parents about the parish schools and fields requests for priestly appearances. While at work, she doesn't think about her finger too much. It is just her left pinkie finger; she can still type seventy-five words a minute. In fact, some people don't even notice it is missing. Those who do usually look appalled and ask, almost reverently, how it happened. Then she has to lie, all the while praying for the Lord to forgive her.

She used to carry the finger with her in a large shoulder bag, the jar wrapped carefully in a bath towel. For a while, she needed it with her all the time. She would take it out at work when no one else was around and in restaurant bathrooms to assure herself that it was still there, that it hadn't dissolved, that the glass of the jar hadn't cracked, leaving it withered and gray. She never showed it to anyone. This was partly because she didn't want anybody to know about it. Cutting it off had been enough to make the nuns expel her from the convent, even though she was, by their account, the most promising novice they'd seen in years. If the fathers found out she had kept it, she would probably be excommunicated. The other reason she never showed anyone is because she was afraid that sharing it would diminish its potency. Her severed finger is a miracle, a divine link. Every time she unwrapped it in the darkness under her desk or in the chill of a bathroom stall, it would glow love. It is a piece of her that is always praying, a sign of the preservative power of God's grace.

She worried so much that she finally stopped carrying it with her. During the day it drifts at the edge of her imagination, two and a half inches of waxy faith suspended in a globe of silvery liquid. At night, she dreams of watery expanses and moons shaped like fingernails.

One Thursday in April, a man in his thirties enters the diocese office a few minutes before closing. He crosses to Rosa's desk and stands in front of her, apparently studying her nameplate. His silence makes her nervous, and she tucks her left hand under her thigh before asking how she can help him. He doesn't speak, and she wonders whether she should try to get past him to the outside door or dash into the copy room behind her where her most lethal weapon would be a five-gallon bottle of toner. Just as she starts to pray to the Lord for divine intervention or at least a little timely guidance, the man pulls a small silver box from his pocket, parts the edges of his collar, and holds the box to the bit of clear tube that protrudes from his throat. "Rosa?"

She thinks it is the most beautiful and terrifying sound she has ever heard. It is a cross between a whisper and a deep bass with overtones of metal, but it is not mechanical. It is a sound she imagines stones make when mating or dying. He repeats, "Rosa?" Again the sound amazes and humbles her, provokes a feeling she has only experienced after praying for hours, late at night, when the other nuns were sleeping and she was alone in the cold arch of the chapel. There is an almost sexual tightening of her abdomen, a powerful contraction deep in her stomach.

"Yes," she whispers.

"I didn't mean to frighten you, it's just that this is the only way …"

He says he has a spiritual problem. His voice still startles her, but she is becoming used to it and its effect on her; however, this question throws her into a panic because all of the priests are out of town for a convention on venial sin except for Father O'Rourke who doesn't approve of conventions and went to Las Vegas instead for the weekend. The man looks distressed by this.

"Well, then maybe you can help me. I guess it is sort of an administrative matter."

"I'm not really an expert," Rosa says. "Don't you think you'd better wait for the fathers to get back?"

The man plucks at his collar in agitation. "If I don't resolve this now, I'm afraid I'll lose my nerve."

She wants to say something reassuring, but her stomach growls and the man smiles and says, "I'm keeping you from your dinner." He holds out his left hand because he is still clasping the silver box to his throat with the right, and she hesitates but finally gives him her left hand to shake and is surprised when he doesn't say anything about her missing finger. That's when she finds herself asking him if he'd like to eat with her at the deli next door so they can talk more about his problem.

Over corned beef and coleslaw he asks about her missing finger, and because he asks so casually, she tells him the truth. He is the first person she has told the story. Everyone else who knows the truth heard it from the nuns who found her in the kitchen, on her knees, her severed finger beside her on the stone floor, her hands clasped, forehead pressed against the avocado metal of the refrigerator. They said she was in *rapture*; the doctors called it shock. She tells him how it didn't bleed at all and how this disappointed her, how even at that time, even when she was having the most meaningful religious experience of her life, she felt somehow cheated by the absence of blood. She tells him without prompting, almost shyly, about the voice she heard before it happened, except it wasn't a voice. It was more a feeling, a shifting of weights and forms around her. That's how she explains it after he asks if she wants cheesecake — it was as if her perception of everything slipped for a moment and she knew what she was supposed to do. He asks only one question.

"What does it mean?"

"It's proof, of course."

It isn't until she has accepted his offer of a ride back to her apartment that she realizes they haven't talked at all about his problem. He is quiet when she reminds him of it. The artificial voice box is a moth, still in his cupped palm. Then he says he was wondering if it was possible to bury objects, not a person, just an inanimate thing, in consecrated ground. She thinks for a long time before she has to say she doesn't know, but she doesn't think so. He sighs when she tells him this. The noise comes from his mouth, not the box; it is a painful sound that makes her knuckles ache. When they reach her apartment, he asks if he can come in for a moment, says that there's something he'd like to show her. And because she feels this bond with him, this recognition, she doesn't even question him, just nods and leads him down the sidewalk to her door.

"Do you have a tape player?"

His voice seems weaker, more metallic than before, and she wonders if he isn't used to talking so much. So, as if her not speaking could conserve his strength, she simply nods again and points to the corner of the living room. He stands in front of the machine for a while, both hands pressed against it. When he does move, it is to reach into his pocket, but this time he brings out a cassette tape, not the silver box. He places it in the deck and presses play, and for a few minutes the room is quiet except for the murmur of the tape cycling into the machine. Rosa is still standing in the entranceway, the door open behind her, and she can see the dark form of his car in the mirror on the opposite wall, and strangely, she can see another reflection within that image. She recognizes the blur of the moon on his windshield as a voice comes out of the speakers and she knows without him telling her, for he is not talking or even looking at her, that this is his voice, was his voice. It is a child singing a song about a spider and a rainstorm, and as the rain starts falling, there is a click where the recording stops.

"May I leave this with you?"

This surprises her but she knows she will say yes, knows she won't be able to help herself, and the sound of the tape player continuing past the voice, scanning silence, brings back that feeling of praying in the empty chapel and another memory, the rasp of metal against stone tile, the smell of onions, the whine a bone makes when it is lost. Rosa wants to give him something in exchange, to show him the thing she holds secret. She says, "I've been keeping something too," and places her left hand on the coffee table, spreads her fingers until they are shaking with the effort, and uses the forefinger of her right hand to trace the cold transparent space where her pinkie used to be.

Last Night of the County Fair

You win a plastic frog at a half-price ring toss, and the hawker urges another game on us, his fingertips stained indigo and trembling. "Something big," he yelps as each ring sails into the air. Across the way, the Ferris wheel endlessly cuts out its steep slice of sky. We've missed the monster trucks and rhinestoned crooners. The crocodile wresting pit is just an oval of damp sawdust. Only the dwarf remains, standing on the gold-painted box, yelling sonnets at the fat lady. A cloud of mosquitoes and pollen and cotton candy fibers balloons above us, some weird blessing. For a moment, I think you are going to propose to me in front of the fry-bread cart, but you are just tying your shoe. Fathers are dragging their children like wounded soldiers over the grass. The Gravitron is still, its doorway a dead mouth exuding the smell of steel and vomit. We are strangers here with the lightbulbs of the concourse burning out one by one overhead. In the corner are the animal sheds and the moldy pies. Someone has cross-stitched the ceiling of the Sistine Chapel onto a pillowcase. In the last stall, there are day-old pigs worming against the big flank of their mother, an FFA project gone unexpectedly exponential. For a moment, I can't remember any dream I've ever had. And look at them; their eyes have yet to open.

A Crown of Sonnets
Dedicated to Long-Gone Love

In this strange labyrinth how shall I turn?
Ways are on all sides while the way, I miss:
If to the right hand, there, in love I burn;
Let me go forward, therein danger is

MARY WROTH

I

The tree outside my window was in bloom. Each morning we would watch its petals, thinking we could see them open. His breath on my left shoulder asking, *when?* Some days we'd lie in bed 'til two with their pinky-white, their paper hearts, their cold stamens—speaking, *soon.* The April silence of that room. My own pink heart was rolling over in my chest, my fingertips were tracing, *when.* Across his chest, across the thin scar where his fifth-grade friend hit him with a leaf-encumbered rake, or maybe it was someone in grad school who carved a letter of her name into him on a whim, an almost "D" that looked more like a spoon.

The flowers on the tree that year were large and frail. I worried when I saw them—their transparent throats it seemed would never turn to plum. The way they shivered under every rain made me think of lightning splitting wood, wrenching dark from pale. He preached the sun; I closed my eyes and saw them dropping one by one. The monsoon season that year was too long— we stayed in bed storm after storm—I learned his skin so well that winter came.

2

Winter came and hovered. And with it, a roll call for my lovers: the sculptor dead, his boot beside the highway, body where? The boy who wrote me songs, whose guitar-calloused palms went dark to fair. And back again depending on the season—at night, dreaming of chords and basketball, those hands would shudder. Next, there was a poet turned to science, and a second poet, and another. And him, the thick turned thin, a starling in my attic (heaven), a single coffee mug, a pair. Him, the one that I misplaced somewhere. Except for him, each one I've lost, I've found again—as with omens, names, healed-over skin, to forget is to discover.

And what about the ones I cannot number? The murky lake beside my house, the fallen tree I used to play on with my brother, with a dark-skinned boy named Tate (he planned to marry me, I said I'd wait) who lived next door. Every single mirror I've passed, the first glossy wasp I killed, the last. That perfect leaf, the saint who weeps in Mexico, the asphalt that softens every summer. All these things that I've called *lover* I've taken in, refused to cede; instead, I've catalogued my greed, been careful to record. But now I find I must ignore the loves I used to grasp, as if my skin can fit no more; I've gorged myself, and now I fast.

3

Too fast he's gone, and then my tooth begins to ache. He's left behind his books, his tapes, the shirt he swears is orange though I insist it's red. I wear it every night to bed. He calls to tell me where he is; I keep a map I mark with foil stars each time he asks me just to *wait*. One month, four months, a year or more—he has me moving state to state. To go to sleep, I count them up; I try to store all fifty in my head. My mouth's too sore; I stay awake and tear the map from end to end. And then I walk the dark rooms of my house and break everything there is that's left to break.

And so the map is gone. For weeks, I've swept up shards of plate or found them in the tough skin of my feet. His shirt has turned to orange again; I do not bother to deny it. Instead I throw it out and buy a few red T-shirts of my own—I wash them twenty times before they start appearing worn. My tooth begins to hurt too much to eat. It's the only thing I keep; it reminds me to stay quiet.

4

Quietly, I count the months, the phantom dates. For him, I'd like a funeral or a wake, some official way to mourn. I do what every other abandoned lover does—I eat too much or not enough, I cut my hair, I turn and turn. While I begin to think that winter will not end, the black-beaked geese pretend to mate. They grapple desperately because they know the wind that segments flock from flock as they push north; I wish I had a heart to break. I wish I had anything besides this mouth to keep me warm. The birds are ugly in their love—wings beat great plumes of dust, every neck is bent or torn. I trust they find some pleasure in it, or some use, though I imagine it's too early still, too soon in their migration lake to lake.

One morning, early, it's still dark, the flock begins to move. I watch them leave, black-studded strands veering into sky; their patterns are incomprehensible, a line of syllables that fade. The sky brightens; they disappear, leaving the ground beneath them desolate. Except for one gray body, wings flung wide, I guess a casualty of love. This bird I envy for its shapely passion, its careless, feather-rending pride, the dull eye it turns upon the water, its beak to earth, sharp as a spade.

5

I shovel dirt upon the bird, and every muscle suffers. I ask the dentist how one is expected to recover from a loss like this, a tooth that one has grown for years. He recommends amalgams, metals, shiny bridges; he says to him it would appear my tooth has died inside my mouth and is now infecting others. He orders X-rays, weighs me down with lead and admonitions to stay covered. I move at first so that the bones are blurs. The next set is perfect; everything is clear, detailed as the stories of mass murders and military coups that I collect for weeks then throw away (or lose) in batches—I trace the small stress fractures. They web my oldest teeth, their patterns surreptitious; the dentist mutters.

He says, *It must come out*. And I agree. But I hesitate to give it over, to sit by patiently while he removes this thing I've carried for so long. He says, *abscess*, *fever*, *implant*, but still I doubt. I meditate on healing as I pay his fee. I schedule an extraction but can't stop touching that disloyal, guilty tooth, can't stop feeling shocked at its defection or imagine it a space, a specially molded crown—my tongue cannot forget despite the dentist's rationale of Novocain and porcelain that something will be gone.

6

Something will be gone, I think as I watch them prep the tray, the
silver tools, the suture thread (milky fine like spider webs), the
flowery deflated gloves. *When pulling teeth, expect a lot of blood*, the
dentist says before he starts. And then he slips the needle in, and
then the dark. I wake, I feel my face; my mouth is numb. The
dentist tells me this is good. He asks what I remember, this part,
this part? I think I heard a saw, a drill, no, the buzzing of my
heart. The dentist keeps on talking, but I am tired—all his words
begin to sound like *love*.

I wake again and search for absence with my tongue. It's there
behind the packing, that black space. I eat ice—the cold's supposed to heal. I feel the chill spread from my throat into my lungs.
I think I can no longer smell or taste the place where my tooth
used to be; an excavation was completed while I slept, while I
dreamt of nothing, well, not nothing—I dreamt of sounds, my
heart, my heart, a gray streak on a page—I dreamt of nothing real.

7

I dream of nothing real. Winter continues to drag out; I move from north to south to hasten its undoing. Even in the desert, things have closed upon themselves, acacias dead, agaves topped by withered plumes. Monsoon rains have warped my door; the swollen wood protects a house in which nothing costs enough to steal. Inside, the dust has formed a shroud, and sunburst widow's webs festoon the windowsills. A black-bulbed spider decorates each room. I leave them there, a charm, a prayer; their poisonous precision soothes. At night, I swear I hear them spinning, each fat egg-sack an axis, the swollen moon the wheel.

The lizards crawling up my walls have changed from clear to rust. I find their bodies in my cupboards ironed flat by dehydration and line them up outside the door in regiments of waiting. Their parched skins rustle, speaking *soon*. I wake one morning to whispers of crenulated claws, the red scent of petals crushed. From my bed, I translate sentences of dust the lizards left behind, a souvenir of their departing. The sun has risen earlier today, and as its tissue-papered light inflames the room, I see the tree outside my window is in bloom.

By the Gleam of Her Teeth,
She Will Light the Path Before Her

After dinner, Father folds a swan out of his paper napkin. Mother says, "My, how early it grows dark." First Daughter laughs at a flickering outside the window. She thinks it is an out-of-season firefly or a spark from the chimney, but really it is someone creeping through the trees with a flashlight.

Father folds triangle over triangle, smaller and smaller, until a head and wings appear. Second Daughter watches the ghost of her grandmother walk around the table and touch everyone's plate. Second Daughter wonders if the dead get hungry and she eats the last corner of her tuna sandwich in one bite so grandmother's ghost will not stand too long by her. Birds fly up from the apple orchard in a cloud blacker than the sky. Only Son screams for his bottle. Mother says, "He has such strong lungs. Perhaps he will be a soldier."

First Daughter goes to the fireplace and pretends to do homework. She writes numbers in long columns and eats the eraser of her pencil in secretive nibbles. Second Daughter follows grandmother's ghost into the kitchen and catches her trying to chew through the rims of cans. Second Daughter wonders if the dead feel pain. She whispers, "Stop," and grandmother's ghost throws a can of pureed tomatoes at her. Father places the swan in the bowl of grapes where it rocks over the uneven fruit and watches everyone out of its mustard-spot eye.

Mother clears the plates from the table. She says, "Goodness, these dishes are so clean, I don't believe they need washing." Father tears Mother's napkin into small pieces. In the garden, rows and rows of green beans tangle closer for warmth. The eggs in the henhouse mutter in their sleep. The light outside the window draws closer. Second Daughter sees it and knows what it is. Someone is moving through the forest toward them.

Only Son screams because grandmother's ghost is biting his upper arm. Mother says, "Perhaps he will be a stockbroker." First Daughter throws her wool mitten into the fireplace to see the yellow smoke. She loves things for the colors they burn. Mother says, "What is that smell?" Grandmother's ghost flies shrieking up the chimney. Second Daughter wonders if the dead can get stuck in small places, and Only Son screams because he is growing older. Father touches the swan's wing with the brown tip of his finger and imagines holding a grape in his cheek, not biting it, just feeling its roundness.

First Daughter wishes she could burn everything. First Daughter wishes she could set her whole body on fire.

Mother says, "When the wind howls like that it means snow." Father pinches the swan's beak so it opens and closes as if repeating Mother's words. Mother and Father both think of the garden and the tender asparagus, which sells for two dollars a bunch. Later, they will have to cover everything in burlap, as if pulling the covers up over their children. Mother remembers her own mother sitting by her bed on fever nights. Mother remembers planning her trousseau, remembers begging for the white silk nightgown, now yellow as an egg yolk in the upstairs closet. Second Daughter points to the window where the flashlight shines. Everyone looks at the window. Mother says, "My, the moon is bright tonight." Only Son screams. He can't remember what moon is, but he thinks it means winter.

Second Daughter imagines all the things that could be circling her house with a flashlight. She remembers stories from school of children being cut up and left in the forest. She remembers the wolves and bears and the abused boys who grow up to torture people found via classified ads. Mother says, "Nonsense, that light is too white to be the moon." Father's brown fingers crush the swan's long throat. The grapes wither a little in their porcelain bowl, roll closer to each other for comfort.

Second Daughter opens the door, and a wind rushes in that is not grandmother's ghost. The light moves away from the window and is lost in the shrubbery. Only Son screams because he knows someday he will sit alone in this same room, hungry and cold. Mother says, "Perhaps he will be a dictator." Father feeds him a grape. First Daughter holds one finger over the fire and then her whole hand. The swan closes its one yellow eye and tries to remember life before dinner. Father sings a lullaby about three thieves and a serial killer. Mother says, "I believe I am getting a chill." Mother says, "No one buys the cow when they can get the milk for free." Only Son moans, and Mother gives him a knife to teethe on. Mother says, "You'll thank me for this later."

Second Daughter walks outside where everything smells like a ghost. She leaves without her red cloak, without her father's ax, without breadcrumbs for the path home. She has only her proud virginity that clangs like a bell, her will to escape like an egg slipping free, and her curiosity, that strange puss, the part of her brain that claws toward the dark. In the night, in the black fringe of the forest, she could be anyone. She could be the witch sipping boy-blood, the doctor scraping lichen for his collection, the girl who runs and runs and runs.

Gravetending

He was a willful child, brown and plump as a loaf of bread, and was left on their doorstep in the middle of the night. When she heard the wailing, Glynnis poked Frank with the crook-handled cane she kept under the bed for burglars. Brother and sister slept in two single beds with white sheets, plain as nuns' beds, the only adornment in the room a chipped red cabinet someone had brought back from China a long time ago. "You hear that?" she asked, thinking it was probably a rabbit caught in a trap or a cat yowling. When Frank came back holding the baby wrapped in the denim workshirt, it was as if the room cracked open from the heat of the infant's angry forehead.

There was no note, nothing except the grease-stained shirt and the child himself, whom they named Lyndon, a name taken from a headstone near the house. A happy name to counter-act the canker, Glynnis thought. A happy grave, always in the sun, covered with a great patch of forget-me-nots that spread like milk over the grass come spring.

They fed the baby with a washcloth dipped in sugar water, as you would a foundling kitten. It was Frank's job to heat the water and test it with his gnarled elbow. They were old when Lyndon came to them, but it was as if they stopped aging that night, as if the steam from the pan of syrup boiling on the stove plumped up all their wrinkles. Glynnis's hair turned dark again and Frank's limp disappeared. Dawn was coming. The baby screamed so hard the stars squinted.

Everyone thought the child was a distant cousin. The brother and sister had no visitors. Glynnis made jam from raspberries that grew in the downhill portion of the graveyard, between the road and the lake. Winters, she made quilts that were sold in the fancy museum in town. It tickled her to think of rich people paying for and sleeping under scraps of her worn-out clothing. The house was a sideways house — white plank, narrow windows — that sat on a strip of lawn between the road and the uphill portion of the graveyard. The hill sloped dramatically up and the graves were terraced, each on their own strip of lawn. There was hardly room for the bodies. Frank and Glynnis knew that many of the caskets were buried into the angle of the hill so that their inhabitants stood up for all eternity. It was Frank's job to dig the graves and cut back the weeds. When the summer storms came, the caskets shifted and holes opened up at the edges of the terrace. Frank tamped earth into the rifts and contemplated the possibility that some day all the caskets would slip down the hill and pop out into the road. Next to the drainage ditch, Glynnis set up an old table and sign and a pyramid of jam jars, three dollars each, honor system.

Lyndon grew up lean, but still brown — brown as a berry, boot leather, the bark of the tree his name mirrored. He went to the village school half days and had a work release, like the kind they give out in prisons, to help Frank tend the graveyard. He learned to subtract from the dates on the headstones; he learned to read from license plates on the cars that shot by the house. He liked geography and arrived at school early to unspool the watery pink and green maps from their rusting shells and trace the vees of the mountain ranges. He could put his finger on any capital city in seconds. The other boys were a bit in awe of this. Geography was an acceptable subject to excel in, unlike music or literature. They called Glynnis a witch and claimed she set her jam with the bones and fingernails of children. Lyndon affected carelessness. He would not be drawn into a fight. If the others shoved him or tore his shirt, his face grew stony and he thought of the Great Salt Lake where even the fattest creatures floated with ease and where the brine shrimp hatched by the millions. The girls in the class cast sidelong glances at him and penned his name over the furrows of their wrists.

At home, they ate mostly fish and bread and bitter greens found by the roadside, boiled down with vinegar and salt. Once in a while, offerings turned up on their doorstep, a wedge of sheep's cheese, a store-bought pie in a foil tin. Glynnis and Frank had no idea why people left things for them; they assumed it had something to do with the cemetery. When Lyndon was a child, Frank taught him how to tie flies and took him to the river to cast. Frank's own father had kept his patterns a secret but had hooked a midge or damsel nymph on his Christmas stocking each year. When their father died, Glynnis found a bank book filled with drawings of flies and notes. Frank buried it in a hole he dug next to his father's grave without opening it. To construct the flies, Frank and Lyndon used horsehair and squirrel tail hair and once, hair from a raccoon run over outside the house. In his pockets, Lyndon kept balls of animal hair that he plucked from the brambles on his way home from school. These hardened into pellets in the wash and Glynnis lined them up behind the framed photos on the mantle, secret trophies. When fishing in the lake, they used bits of rotting meat that Frank kept in a Tupperware in the refrigerator for this purpose. They cleaned the fish on the shore and the entrails floated in the rocking water. It was from Frank that Lyndon learned augury by guts and bird formations. Early snows and droughts and frosts were unmistakable in the scrawl of the geese flying overhead and the drift of the intestines. The weeks before Lyndon had appeared on the doorstep, all the birds had flown in clusters of three.

One morning, during the hour on local history, the other boys wrote *Vampire* in marker on the back of his jacket that was hanging from his chair. This was one of their riffs, that Frank was one of the undead, that he slept in the graveyard and rose up each night to suck the blood of the local livestock. Skinny, old, shambling Frank! With his drooping trousers and his quiet voice and the sandy hairs covering his arms. Lyndon wished Frank was a vampire; he wished all the cattle would drop dead simultaneously. Glynnis always ended the story of his arrival at their door as an infant by declaring that there were some things thicker than blood. She said this like a joke but always patted him on the head when she said it, even now that he was a grown boy. Lyndon told her he had lost the jacket on a field trip to the state legislature and went cold the rest of the winter.

Frank liked to read books about far-off places, especially the parts about how the dead were treated. At dinner, he described urns of oil and honey, packets of food, candies in the shapes of skulls, blankets of marigolds and scores of clay servants. He said that in Vietnam, they built a hut over the grave and then replaced it a few years later with a wood house, nice as anything the living occupied. In Poland, there was a flurry of scrubbing of stone once a year, and flower sellers crowded the roads to the cemeteries. Some places, they built elaborate shrines at the graves and left pictures of new babies and pets, bowls of rice, candles, and little statues of birds and frogs. He had seen a photo of a tomb in New Orleans with a wrought-iron fence and a pile of bottles of whisky. They looked out the window at the quiet graveyard as they ate. A flag fluttered at one headstone; on another a blanched plastic wreath clattered. Beyond the graves, over the heap of the mountain, cows and horses grazed, and beyond that, teenage boys lay on their beds, drinking orange juice out of the carton, reading books about men who could fly.

During the years Lyndon studied geology at a neighboring branch of the state college, he still lived with Glynnis and Frank and still dug the weeds out of the cemetery every May. One winter afternoon, the day after a storm which dumped three feet of snow on the graves, Frank had a heart attack while Lyndon was in class learning about mass wasting. His professor explained the slow process of downhill creep, the affecting factors of soil type and vegetation and precipitation, and chalked on the board, *angle of repose*. Lyndon thought of the graves inching down the hill. When he came home that night, hands chapped from gripping the steering wheel against the icy roads, Glynnis had prepared nothing for dinner. Frank was in the hospital two towns over, and Glynnis and Lyndon sat at the splintery kitchen table and ate slice after slice of toast, laden with jam, as if they could not get enough sweetness to fill them. Glynnis told Lyndon that Frank was fated to die first because he was a man, because men's hearts are so big and unruly. Lyndon knew Frank had a girlfriend in town that he saw on Sundays, the day of the week the inhabitants of the sideways house turned invisible. Summers, Frank's girlfriend worked at the museum where Glynnis's quilts were sold, dressed in calico and churning butter. "Good money," she always said when Frank put on her bonnet to tease her. He never brought her home; she said grave-yards creeped her out because she didn't know where to stand. She didn't go to visit him in the hospital because it was winter and her bonnet was packed away. Glynnis, at the kitchen table, sur-rounded by empty jam jars, claimed her own heart was small as a walnut and thumped her chest so hard tears sprang into her eyes.

So it was a surprise when Glynnis died first, later that year, at the beginning of summer, when the leaves were still so tender Lyndon wished he was a deer. The doctor said she was riddled with cancer and charged sixty dollars to sign the death certificate. Frank died two days later from a massive heart attack while fishing with Lyndon. He flung his arm up to cast and hitched on the backstroke, sending the hook wildly into the air where it caught Lyndon on the earlobe and tore. Both men cried out in pain and Frank crumpled into the river, growing so sodden and heavy that Lyndon struggled to drag him out. It was only when Lyndon saw them laid out in the funeral parlor, side by side, that he realized they were twins. Frank's black wool suit and Glynnis's black wool dress were both too small for the corpses because they shrank in the dryer at the town laundromat where Lyndon had hurriedly washed them. It gave the illusion that the siblings were still chil-dren, outgrowing their clothes faster than anyone could afford. No one came to the viewing and there was no funeral; Glynnis's will stipulated cremation and scattering anywhere but the ceme-tery. The box Lyndon carried back to the house was flesh-colored plastic. Inside, the ashes were in a cellophane bag with a red-and-white-striped twist tie he recognized from bags of supermarket bread. He put the box in the kitchen window facing the road and went through the house, looking for secrets.

In the twins' bedroom he found two pairs of Frank's shoes. One scraped and worn through at the toe and one still in the box. The acrid scent of tanned leather and polish filled the room when Lyndon opened the lid. Glynnis's one pair of shoes, black leather lace-ups, had been burnt up with her. Under her bed, in a brittle dress box from the now-defunct department store in town, there was an assortment of linens with hand-crocheted trim and a blank space for the monogram. A virgin's hope chest. The pillowcases and tablecloths were white and fresh-smelling. She must have aired them in the sun each year and tucked them away again. The red Chinese cabinet had many awkwardly-sized drawers and a top that popped up as a vanity. The mirror was cracked, three jagged lines and one wedge missing. Lyndon could not recall when this had happened. He remembered Glynnis bouncing him in front of the mirror, the only one in the house except for Frank's pocket shaving mirror on the shelf in the bathroom. *This is how the gentleman rides.* The drawers were filled with screws and nails, old paper dolls, clippings from newspapers that seemed to have no unifying theme (a recipe for arthritis liniment, a letter to the editor about speed limits), calico scraps for a rag rug, shellacked red paper poppies from years of memorial days, two letters from their mother to their father when he went to a livestock auction out of town (*I love you, dearest. The corn is higher than I've ever seen it.*), loose keys without markings, a Dixie cup filled with crumbling rubber bands. In the bottom drawer, their birth certificates, frayed at the folds. They both had their mother's maiden name, Southby, as their middle name. Lyndon could not think where else to look. The Chinese cabinet was the only closed piece of furniture in the house. In his room, a small nook wedged between the bathroom and the stairs, he traced the frets of his childhood and adolescent heights marked in pencil on the door-frame. He peered at the window to see where he had scratched his initials into the corner of the glass. On the floor, there was a large gouge where he had dragged the bed away from the wall the autumn he was afraid of ghosts. The bench at the end of the bed was piled with the quilts Glynnis had made for him over the years, *wishing quilts* she had called them, star-patterned, intricate as any map, corduroy-backed. Downstairs, there was nothing, just the usual sand in the corners of rooms, an inexplicable row of furry pellets on the mantle, the shelf of his textbooks, all marked in other people's handwriting. Rows and rows of jam jars stood proudly in the window, casting a red glow over the kitchen. They would last him years. It appeared he had been left at their door as a baby, hungry and anonymous, just as they had always told him.

Lastly, he went outside to examine the stoop. There was a cake and a foil pan of meatloaf on it. There was also a wreath of daisies interwoven with white clusters of wild dill. Ladybugs were swarming over it. The stoop itself was a substantial ledge of limestone worn down in the middle by years of stepping. He felt all the fibers of his unruly heart unwind as he looked at the infant-sized depression in the step. Every Saturday, Glynnis had lugged a kettle of boiling water outside to scrub the stoop. In the winter, the steam rose up in clouds. A trowel was rusting in the grass. Frank had been meticulous about his tools and the only time he had ever struck Lyndon was when the boy had left out a pickaxe all night in the rain. In the lean-to that held the shovels and rakes,

Lyndon sanded the rust from the trowel blade and oiled it. The oil can clicked satisfyingly and gave off a happy scent that was part automobile, part eucalyptus.

On his way back into the house, he gathered up the food and the flowers. The door closed behind him with a solid clap. There was no echo. A hundred mountains stood before him, but he couldn't imagine their coordinates. He was thinking about the gift of dinner, the way a car's headlights lit up the kitchen like a shrine at night, the planet traveling and him with it, surrounded by all he knew.

In Your Endeavors,
You May Feel My Ghostly Presence
(Instructions for Contacting the Dead)

Based on fragments from *The Forms of Water in Clouds
and Rivers, Ice and Glaciers* by John Tyndall

Trace a river to its source.

Go to the mouth of the river Rhone. Go to the head of the lake.
Pass these and push your journey still higher.

I will act as your guide. I, who am recently blown out, undone,
plunged into darkness.

Look to your bedroom windows when the weather is very
cold outside.

Through that clear space the thing must pass.

Light a fire, fuse metal, or burn the hand like a hot solid.

We must now be observant.

Dip your finger into a basin of water and cause it to quiver
rapidly to and fro.

Imagine a southwest wind. Note the consequence.

Supposing, then, that we withdraw.

You have already noticed I entertain an affection, a passion, a desire for company. I warn you: I wish.

If in a dark room, you close your eyes and press the eyelid with your fingernail, a circle of light will be seen opposite to the point pressed, while a sharp blow upon the eye produces the impression of a flash of light.

The shock of little waves.

Imagine them placed at a distance from each other and perfectly free to move.

You may feel (when the hoarfrost is removed), you may feel the dark waves, the air, the blind forces of nature, a delicate shimmer of blue light, a sound like thunder, the abstract idea of a boy.

What, then, is this thing which at one moment is transparent and invisible and at the next moment visible?

To return blow for blow. Almost transparent to others. A delicate balance. Not so perfect as the first.

Every occurrence in Nature is preceded by other occurrences that are its causes and succeeded by others that are its effects.

Pour cold water into a dry drinking glass on a summer's day.

You may observe a luminous body, the existence of which you were probably not aware.

It is necessary that you should have a perfectly clear view of this process.

Take a slab of lake ice and place it in the path of a concentrated sunbeam.

Through that clear space the thing must pass.

Thus by tracing backward our river from its end to its real beginnings we come at length to the sun, the abstract idea of a boy.

Prove this, if you like.

Fold two sheets of paper into two cones and suspend them with their closed points upward.

Could my wishes be followed out, I would at this point of our researches carry you off with me.

When the red sun of the evening shines upon these cloud-streamers, they resemble vast torches with their flames blown through the air.

But it is quite plain that we have not yet reached the real beginning of rivers.

Fill a bladder about two-thirds full of air at the sea level and take it to the summit of Mont Blanc.

Hence it is the dark waves, the heat of these waves, the truth of the statement, sending a smoke of spray into the air. Hence the wisdom of darkening.

Is this language correct?

You have already noticed. No effect whatever is produced.

It is necessary to employ the obscure heat of a body raised to the highest possible state of incandescence.

This has been observed in Russian ballrooms.

Supposing, then, mutually attracting points. Waves competent to burn the hand like a hot solid.

An ascending current rises from the heated body.

Feel the heat of these waves with your hand. Get upon the ice and walk upward. The truth of the statement made in paragraph 34 is thus demonstrated.

And you have the Fire-Balloon. A body, almost transparent to others, may exist in a perfectly dark place.

Allow a sunbeam to fall upon a white wall in a dark room. Bring a heated poker, a candle or a gas flame underneath the beam.

Oddly enough, though I was here dealing with what might be called the abstract, I desired. I had descended the glacier, leaping with indescribable fury from ledge to ledge.

If the experiment be made for yourself alone, let the air come to rest and then simply place your hand at the open mouth.

A delicate shimmer of light, a sound like thunder, a dense opaque cloud, a perfectly dark place, which, through some orifice that it has found or formed, comes to the light of day.

A body, a break, a sharp blow. Can you see me? Can you feel my breath? My tortured heat?

But we cannot end here. We have sought to reveal more.

The point of disturbance, the end of a delicate balance, a luminous body. The shock of little waves.

We must exist.

This is the point to which I wished to lead you and without due preparation could not be understood.

We cannot end here.

I had descended the glacier, a break in the chain of occurrences,
a body raised to the highest possible state, consciously warm
and real.

My object thus far is attained. I have given you proofs (a slab
of lake ice, a dry drinking glass, the Fire-Balloon). Resolution
must not be wanting.

We can have refreshment in a little mountain hut.

I should have told you. I am describing your own condition.
Imperfect, a dark room, incandescence, and then, the hoarfrost
that cannot be removed.

I should have told you rain does not come from a clear sky.
I should have told you a sharp blow is necessary for a flash of
light. I should have told you this thing which at one moment
is transparent and invisible and at the next moment visible
is not so perfect as the first.

I desired to keep you fresh as well as instructed, untouched,
without any break. It is thus I should like to teach you all things.
But it is quite plain you may feel, you may feel the darkening,
a source of agitation, the shock of little waves.

It is not, therefore, without reason I warned you against
entering. The hoarfrost cannot be removed.

And you and I have shivered thick bomb-shells into fragments.

A break in the chain of occurrences. I wish, I wish.... But you have already noticed the wreathing and waving of the current, the deep soft sand, the whirling eddies, a southwest wind.

You have already noticed the reproach to the body, the unstoppable plunge toward a perfectly dark place. You cannot halt it for me any more than you can for yourself.

Should we not meet again, the memory of these days will still unite us. Or rather, was not the paying of the price a portion of the delight?

Give me your hand, note the consequence, the obscure heat of a body. You alone must pass through that clear space.

The Woman Who Fell
in Love with a Meteorologist
and Stopped the Rain

She watches him every night at 10:12. When he says dewpoint, she breaks into a sweat, and it is as if her body has stolen the moisture of his mouth as he pronounces those two syllables. He is not particularly handsome, but as he moves before a map of the United States, pointing out cold fronts and low-pressure systems, she thinks he looks like an angel in a button-down shirt wielding a battered steel pointer instead of a sword.

He is an old-fashioned man, the kind of man who would tighten the fan belt of her car when it needed it and take out the trash and reach for the high things in the pantry. Not only the pointer gives him away, but also the way he fumbles with the remote that changes the views of cloud cover and frontal boundaries and the way he fixes his gaze just a bit to the left of the camera, clearly puzzled by the miniature of himself in the monitor superimposed upon invisible geography.

In severe weather, he is disconcertingly spontaneous, appearing unexpectedly in the middle of a soap opera shootout or a talk show featuring exotic animals. These are intimate moments;

his hair is mussed, his shirt untucked. Red patches blush the satellite images as he urges her to take cover and watch for downed trees. She knows exactly what he smells like: Xerox toner and lemons. And she imagines how she will rub her body with crushed grass and cobwebs, blueberries and road salt so that he can map the seasons in the dark.

This is not a love story. If it were, there would be a certain pathos in a woman conjuring a lover out of storm watches and tornado warnings. It is instead a fairy tale, where two people can live in imaginary worlds, bounded only by the limits of the blue screen, clutching remote controls in harmony, and achieve perfect happiness in the four minutes and thirty seconds that they coincide each evening. That is, they could if it weren't for the complication of a garden.

On Thursday, wearing a halo of dots marked Boise, Chicago, and Albany, he predicts rain for the weekend. She has seven rows of split-cup daffodils that have been waterlogged by three weeks of storms. They are the last in a succession of many years of failures. Each fall, she plants the bulbs with a sense of banked hope that lasts on the promise of creamy-lipped petals and crimson hearts through the subzero temperatures and deep snows of winter until soggy spring and early summer when she excavates the barren plots to find bulb after bulb, rotten and swollen with milky pus. Obviously, her garden needs better drainage. In lieu of this, she wills it not to rain.

Friday, he nervously predicts rain again and reminds her to take an umbrella to the weekend's Little League game. She imagines her bulbs floating like heads in the ruin of her garden and steels herself against him. It is their first quarrel, and it takes the pleasure out of the sight of his solid figure against the cartoon graphics of the five-day forecast.

That weekend there is no rain, and she finds small, tentative green hairs in the dirt of her backyard. Sunday night, he is jocular and somewhat abashed but with bird-wing gestures and subtropical magic, calls up a storm for the beginning of the week. She ignores the disapproving swirls of cloud on the Doppler scan and fantasizes forty-two spikes of color.

It is so dry and warm the next few days that the mud hardens and cracks and a full two inches of split-cup daffodil emerge. By 10:12 p.m. on Tuesday, he is pale and thinner but doggedly insists on storm patterns and imported Canadian air. She visualizes her flowers basking in the heat and sends the jet stream spinning northward, away from her garden.

As the week progresses, he grows more stubborn in his pronouncements. She feels a twinge over tricking him like this, like the wife who tosses her husband's favorite ratty sweatshirt and insists he has misplaced it. But the lines of green tongues tasting the air of her garden remind her of imbalance of their relationship, the way he has never had to wait for her, how he doesn't know the tense pleasure of anticipation.

Wednesday it does not rain. Thursday it does not rain. On Friday, he is hoarse and shadowy as he traces storm systems and bungles computer overlays. As she watches him invoking humidity and cloud crystals, she finds regret deep like a stone in her throat and gives up willing the sun.

All weekend she waits for rain. She sits outside trying to detect clouds against the pure blue until her eyes burn and the weight in her chest blossoms into full-blown remorse. Her daffodils grow under the painfully clear sky in seven arches of reproach.

Sunday, he says thunderstorms and heavy showers, and she tries God and St. Swithun, the patron saint of rain, praying they will send another deluge and not disgrace the man who lives four and a half minutes each night to plot His terrible path in precipitation and hard freezes. Monday, she stands barefoot in the garden, her toes curled into the earth to hold her in place as she waters forty-two bright needles of shame.

Three more nights he asserts rain. He is gray and wrinkled from the effort, and his hands shake beneath the weight of his sincerity. She can see the egg-white streaks of the high-resolution radar tracking system showing through his dark-jacketed midsection, and when he gasps the words *moist air*, she feels the impact of his breath on her forehead and the coolness of her tears as they evaporate into the expanse between the sofa and the television set.

By Thursday, he has disappeared. A young man with perky hair and blanched-almond teeth who used to do the Sunday sports highlights hovers in his place. She switches off the set at 10:13 and goes outside. Beneath the heavy curve of the moon, the daffodil stalks are sturdy slashes.

There might be a moral here. But it is nothing so simple as the impossibility of holding onto two imaginary things at once, a lover and a garden. It is a more difficult thing she is feeling as she stands outside in the dark, difficult in the way a daffodil bulb is difficult, gnarled and secret. The truth is, she never really could picture him here. He existed in rectangular spaces, and her garden is humpbacked and sprawling, irregular, unkempt, maybe the shape of her heart.

This Is a Love Story, Too

This morning, when the rooster would not stop crowing and the first egg I cracked had a bloody yolk, I knew. Now the sun is rising to the end of its tether. Soon, it will be on its way down, and the woods will darken first.

No one cares about the old lady. I was like that myself, before I became the old lady. They leave their offerings on the doorstep and sometimes they come in and beg a story and then I am in the newspaper again, the tired gory details dredged up anew, wrinkled black and white, a photo I search for signs of my former self.

She is moving toward me today—I can feel her, the flame of her, her trotting steps, the basket swinging on her arm.

Even today, I have my chores, so I lace up my tennis shoes and peg the clothes on the line. The sheets bell like sails; the monogram on them is not mine. The weeds are choking the vege-table patch, and I drag them up by the roots. I can be ruthless. I wring chicken necks and drown unwanted kittens. I shot a raccoon last July because he wouldn't leave my trash cans alone. Once, I stepped on a nail that went all the way through the meat of my foot and I just pulled it out and walked on. I birthed three children in the cottage bed, and only one of them lived. In the black earth above the other two, I planted peonies whose heads I cut each spring for my kitchen table. My mother used to say that it was the little things that killed you. My mother told me to tread gently in the woods.

She is closer now. I can feel her. She is a berry, the glossy poison kind. She is the one I care about, not him, all teeth and talk. She is the important one, flesh of my flesh. Who knew that blood could be so greedy? I want to see her, no matter what comes next. I want to see her plump cheeks, her shining eyes, and drink my fill. It is the one thing denied to me, I think, if I'm reading the story right.

When it was my turn, I took the basket eagerly enough. The leaves chattered in the spring wind. The path was soft under my feet. The hood was warm and fleece-lined, and I was clean as a river stone underneath, fresh-shaven, flossed, exfoliated and moisturized. I was more toothsome than the cakes I carried and I knew it. When he appeared, I wasn't surprised, but I could not look away from his mouth. I loved the way he smoked his cigarette down to the very end. Why didn't his fingers burn? Why didn't the whole forest light?

All my married life I wondered which I had ended up with—the wolf or the man with the ax.

This is what I know: there is a cloak bright as a geranium muffled in my closet, the bloodstains dark at the hem; when he talks to her, she cannot help but listen; I will make a flourless torte, the chocolate one with the bourbon, as if this were my birthday; the end will not be painless for any of us.

All those years ago and still I can hear his voice, the growl of it, *Hey, baby*. He called me *chickadee* as if I were small and harmless. He ate the cakes with both hands, and I carried an empty basket through the woods.

Ah, the old lady, the old lady. There is no escaping her. She hangs out the wash and stokes the fire. She makes up the bed with the sun-scented sheets. She gasps a little when she catches her reflection in the silver teapot. The teapot shows her the truth; there is an infinite sequence of her, like a nesting doll or a line of dominoes set on end.

I am too old to believe in fairy tales. I feel the glow of her on the dim path to my clearing and I know I'll never see her face. He is the one who will come to me. Again. But this time there will be no endearments. He, or the other one, the woodsman with his musty barn jacket, will proffer it all to her. They are the ones she will thank as she walks through the cottage, touching the gravy boat and the polished stones of the fireplace. She will have never seen such objects in her life. The painting of the ship at sea will stop her in her tracks as she tries to name the exact color of the waves. I have things I would tell her, messages I can leave only in the most homely of ways. *Oh, baby*, I would say. *Chickadee*. Hang up your cloak next to mine, next to the others. See the place on the floor where the blood has fallen? You must scrub it with sand to get the stain out. The sheets will bleach in the sun. I've given you everything, the clear days, the smell of smoke in his hair, all the plates and tins and implements. There are morning glories hidden behind the chicken coop. Whichever one you end up with, never tell him the truth about the other—there are some things that shouldn't be said aloud. The pump handle sticks, but when the water gushes out, it is cold as sin and twice as delicious. Strawberries grow in the shade at the edge of the forest—you have to hunt for them.

Now. He lifts the latch, and the door swings open. My mother used to say there was no time like the present. I step forward like a bride. He knows all my soft parts. Still some way off in the woods, I see it, the ruby scrap, a cardinal flitting perhaps, the reflection of the setting sun. I keep my eyes on it, ignoring him as if he were a doctor prodding me, a paper sheet between us. I watch until the red fills my vision, seeping up from my very skin.

How to Remember a Bird

There is a hole growing in the center of town. People come from all over to see it. The first time anyone noticed, it was the size of a pumpkin, but since then, it has become so big we have stopped measuring. Just last month, the bakery slipped into it, and for days, the hole smelled like rye bread. It is hard to tell when the hole is going to open wider, so we don't get too close to its edges. Of course, children are fascinated by the hole and must be kept away with warnings and threats. My friends and I used to stand near the edge of the hole and dangle our heads over. It was a strange feeling, as if something were both pushing and pulling us, a feeling that we could endure only for a few moments, just long enough to start to see the outlines of things rumbling below us and to hear the echo of conversations, so faint they might have just been our own voices, reflected.

A few years ago, a paleontologist from St. Louis came looking for bones and fell in. He caught hold of a root (*gnarled as an old woman's knee*, he said later) and held himself there, about twenty feet down, until some men from the filling station pulled him out with a rope. He is the only person I can remember who went into the hole and came back out. Before he left to go north and look at something frozen, he told us that in the hole he saw armchairs and tennis racquets sticking out of the walls and heaps of shoes and staplers piled onto ledges. I think it changed him, being in there, because he didn't talk about rock strata and geologic eras anymore. He couldn't stop describing items he spotted and sounds he heard and how dark the center of the hole was, how it was like night, except in pieces he felt moving against him. We listened to him carefully because a lot of the things he mentioned were familiar, things we had lost a long time ago.

When anyone dies in the town, we say that person went into the hole. Even the older townspeople say it, though they knew a time when there wasn't a hole and still there was death. Last Fourth of July, the oldest woman in town gave a speech about when we didn't have the hole and how life was worse then. She said having a hole was a way of remembering. But a lot of people didn't believe her and called her senile. When I was young, my parents told me our cat, Galileo, went into the hole, but I saw them putting her in the metal drum where we burned trash out in the yard. That was when I realized there were several ways into the hole. I found another in the back of Brian McConner's Volkswagen bus, where I had sex for the first time. There was a little refrigerator that Brian had painted with neon green daisies, and as we slid and slipped all over the foam mattress that smelled of patchouli and sweat, those daisies went translucent and dark, disappearing before my very eyes. Years later, the paleontologist described neon flowers glowing deep in the hole, almost covered by junk mail and half-empty nail polish bottles, flourishing like some strange plant that only existed thirty-five feet underground.

It is said that if you throw something from a dream into the hole, the dream will leave you forever and a new one will come in its place. For instance, if Bill, the diner owner, throws his apron into the hole he'll spend his nights combing the tail of a piebald horse instead of washing endless mounds of gravy-crusted dishes. And if the horse's spots look curiously porcelain and the comb is spongy, that is not the hole's fault. Young girls throw their brothers' knives and their fathers' keys and their grandmothers' glasses into the hole and go home to dream of sailcloth and hiking boots and bicycle tires. I've tried it myself. I've dreamed the death of Mrs. Pritchard's son and a tree falling on the barbershop and a best friend sinking in the mud of another country, all in exchange for a hair that was left in my bed. The dreams you get are not always happy ones, merely someone else's and by virtue of that, never nightmares.

Last week, a news crew from Los Angeles came to do a story on our hole. They interviewed the mayor and the town beauty who was second runner-up for Miss America two decades ago. They also interviewed my mother because she is the organizer of the anti-hole faction in town, and she argued the necessity for a fence or dynamite, something to stop its growth. And they interviewed me because I am the town historian, a position that pays surprisingly well in a town with a hole. The reporter was brittle and had only eight beautiful teeth, the four front teeth on the top and the bottom. The rest shone pewter in the cave of his mouth, but when he held the call-sign-emblazoned microphone before his lips, the women of the town swooned. Between takes, girls offered him coffee and kisses, and matrons presented him with pies and floury eyelash flutters. While they flocked around him, I examined the cameraman who slouched in the background. He had floppy hair that covered one eye and a baggy sweater that hung past his fingertips. He also had bulky black headphones, loops of blue and red cord festooning him, and the mouth of a Caravaggio angel. While I was being interviewed I couldn't keep from staring at him, and when the segment aired, it looked as if I was startled by the attention and lights, when really I was plotting a course for those lips that started at my jaw and ended at the turn of my ankle.

It is hard to describe the hole. Digging into a backyard is not enough. A tear in a shirt is closer to the truth, something that shifts, something you can see skin through. When people who don't live here come to see the hole, they always want it to be explained. The town council tried to raise money for a kiosk with a tape player and a recording, but they weren't very successful. We all knew it was only a matter of time before the kiosk fell into the hole, and some people didn't like to imagine the tape player down there. They thought it would be a waste of a voice.

For the news crew, I talked about the time my mother was a teenager drinking a lime phosphate in the drugstore and half of the building disappeared into the earth. I tried to tell it like she did, using my hands to outline the shape of soda glasses and wincing at the sharp taste of lime, but I added things like rows of licorice, black as beetles behind the counter, and the way she sat there to finish her drink, even the thick syrup at the bottom.

What I didn't say is how the hole looks when it opens suddenly, or what happened to the pewter-mouthed reporter. Other news crews came to town to discover what had happened to the first. Of course, I knew what happened to them; it is my business to know. And as with so many stories, there are two versions. In one, the reporter asks me to take some night shots by the hole, to act as filler for the interviews, he says. At night, the hole seems to breathe. And as I stand by the hole with the reporter, translating its burps and sighs for him, he, perhaps because I am the one woman in town not offering him anything, clutches my breasts and presses his eight good teeth against my mouth. I can't step back because the hole is behind me, and for a moment I am placid in his grasp, until I open my eyes and see the cameraman, still filming, those perfect lips curving. It is then that I feel the hole stirring, as if it is offended on my behalf. I unlatch myself from those unnatural teeth and hands and step to the side, and there is time while I'm inching away from the edge to say something. But I don't say anything at all, don't call out a warning, despite the reporter's microphone jutting toward me, the microphone which, by virtue of its cord, drags the cameraman down with the reporter as the hole suddenly widens. And I don't say anything about it to the police or the news crews that come looking for them because I expect they will pop up somewhere else if they haven't already, a miracle of teeth and lips emerging from the soil in Thailand or Baghdad, bruised and dusty but with the camera rolling.

There is another version of the story that I also don't tell. It is midmorning, during a lull between thunderstorms, and I am walking near the hole when a crow flies over it. The crow is so black and large I stop to watch it, and it seems for a moment that I can see the hole reflected in the shiny feathers of its chest. It is a beautiful bird. Just as it reaches the air directly over the hole, I feel the ground shake. But *shake* is not the right word—it is more a recoiling or a reaching, something involuntary. And when I look down at the hole, it moves. It is hard to explain; there is a hole moving somewhere, but it may not be the one in front of me. It may be a hole somewhere else, opening for the first time. It may be a lie or a thwarted desire or a deadline expiring. This is one of the reasons I haven't told the story to anyone, because I don't have proof. I can only say, one day I was walking after a rainstorm and saw a piece of a hole flying over me.

Another reason I don't tell the story is because tourists don't want to hear things like that. They enjoy tales of farmers pulling people out of the ground and bakeries being destroyed. I'd like to show them the birthmark spreading over my ribs when they ask for directions to the hole. I'd like to explain where a hole lives, how it can fit under a fingernail or inside a word. If I were making the recording for the kiosk, I would have it say a *hole is something you give to someone you love, and a hole is a pear, and a hole is the bruise you got while playing kickball in the fifth grade* until everyone understood. But the truth is that people can't believe as easily in a hole as they do in a lime phosphate. Even black holes, so strong they absorb light, seem like figments of our imaginations. And yet, some scientists spend their entire lives studying these faraway things they will never be able to touch or taste. The townspeople who side with my mother would like to fill the hole with tons of dirt and gravel. I've spent innumerable town meetings explaining that a hole is not something to be filled; there is no way to do it. The only thing to do with a hole is to take measurements and photograph it and tell it over and over. And to stand next to it, regularly, as close as possible.

There Is a Factory in Sierra Vista
Where Jesus Is Resurrected Every Hour in
Hot Plastic and the Stench of Chicken

Stand still. I am taking your picture.

The mission behind you, the sky paralyzed turquoise, the stop
sign and the gleaming tourist cars, the way your hair is too long
at the neck.

You said when you called, "It's worth a try."

You have a voice so seductive men have ridden twenty extra
blocks on city transit to continue hearing it.

I winced when you said "miracles."

The chipped metallic green of your Plymouth. The sound the
tires made on the smooth skin of the highway.

The four sentences in a row you started with maybe while
I calculated mileposts.

The way you wash everything twice.

I have counted the moles on your breasts: 7. I have counted the moles on my breasts: 3.

As we hike up the hill to the mission, you are breathing too hard.

My grandfather used to bring me here at Christmas, at Easter, to pray to the saints even though we were Methodist.

The night we hid in your mother's pantry and ate jalapeño-flavored sea kelp crackers and told stories about the perversions we had tried so far.

I called you whore because you let men buy you things.

The thirty-two freckles that ring my neck. One for each year.

Blue line in the employee bathroom, ochre metal stall door, rotten sweet smell of discarded maxi-pads present like a charm.

On our drive here, I asked what you would wish for and you said, "anything."

A plaque on the hillside that lists the names of dead nuns.

The first gift you ever gave me: a baby tooth I keep in my wallet.

When I told you about it, I said, "I nearly fainted." I said, "But I was so careful," and we laughed at how trite we had become.

The desert smells like creosote and gasoline.

The mission large and white before us. You stop to have a cigarette.
I look for a pattern to the dark lines rain has left in the stucco.

The ghosts we saw that whole year we were fourteen.

The legend goes: when the cat that is carved over the door
of the chapel catches the mouse that is carved next to it, the
world will end.

You say, "Someday you can show her how I taught you to waltz."
You touch my wrist as you say it.

You smoke Pall Malls because your first boyfriend did.

On the dirt road from the highway, palo verde trees leaned to
touch us.

A fry-bread stand. A gift store. A mission tilting in the background.

When you told me about your two dead lovers and your
bleeding gums, I said, "So, get tested." I said, "I'll go with you.
I'll bring donuts."

You pose me next to the fountain shaped like a fish, a pale
blurred arc over the sand.

Virgin Mary coasters and powdered sugar.

You called me "slut" because I let men buy me things.

Last week, a man went out into the desert and shot holes into
a saguaro until it fell over and crushed him.

The way you slather honey and sugar on fry-bread.

I know it is too soon to feel anything moving, but there is a
flickering inside me.

Country music coming from the transistor radio in the gift store.
A magnet cut into Jesus on the cross, red rhinestone chips for
blood.

Hand-lettered signs that lined the dirt road.

I say, "That shit will kill you."

The guy who works at the video store and wears shiny too-tight
cowboy shirts, whose mouth tried to chew away the poppy seed
trail of my freckles.

Crooked acrid marker letters spelling, *Happiness is submission
to God*.

When we were kids playing fatal disease, you always had
cancer; I always died for love.

The photo that will show us standing next to a plaster fish,
how scared we look even with our mouthfuls of fry-bread and
movie-star sunglasses.

Your long fingers sorting tiny arms and legs and houses. *Milagros*. Miracles. Hammered tin in the shape of wishes.

The way you squint when you lie.

I buy two thick translucent candles for $1.50 each. You buy one of the small metal hearts.

The second gift you gave me: half of a blood orange that your mother bought by mistake.

My bookcase arranged alphabetically. Your T-shirts ordered by color.

The gift store woman hands you change. I ask what you will wish for and you say, "a pure heart."

The mission, white and lined and heavy-doored.

Afternoon.

My chest aches from the heat.

You kiss my cheek and leave a honey imprint that itches as it dries.

When you told me about it, I said, "Two dead lovers are no proof." I said, "Why do you always have to outdo me?"

Our hands touching as we pull the door wide, benediction of cool air.

The year you painted the same picture fifteen times and I killed
six ficus trees.

You say, "How old is this guy anyway?"

Holy water fingerprints stinging our foreheads, saints scaling
adobe walls wearing red and white satin.

The way you talked too loud as you drove us here. The way
I could still hear the pavement groaning beneath us.

On the left, a statue of St. Francis, lying on his back, so small
and withered.

The summer we were virgins and your brother caught us kissing
in your backyard.

Another flicker, somewhere lower.

A bank of candles, lighting and unlighting themselves over
and over.

You said as we turned off the highway, "So, how does it feel,
this thing growing inside you?"

The places you touch St. Francis: his neck, his thighs,
his stomach.

The matching Celtic knots we were going to get tattooed on our hipbones until we decided to buy each other diamond earrings instead.

Recorded tour whispering from small cheap speakers.

The day you came to my house crying because asparagus was out of season and I sang Johnny Cash songs to you until my throat hurt.

Your fingers sifting through the clusters of snapshots, *milagros*, notes, and hospital bracelets that shroud St. Francis.

The black tuxedo pants that we both have, the Mondays we swim at the Y.

Bells chime four o'clock. The candles fade and brighten.

When we were driving here you asked what I would wish for and I said, "Enough rain to make mud, something we can sink into." You said, "Be serious."

I light both of our candles with your lighter.

The recording starts over.

How we laugh at women who wear bikinis, how we smirk when someone says love.

The month you wouldn't talk to me. The winter you slept on
my couch.

I hold your candle upside down to catch the flame until three
pale drops scald my wrist.

The brown scarf you loaned me that I never gave back.

How you pretended to cough all the way from Tucson until I said,
"You can stop that. I know you aren't really dying."

The girlie magazines we used to steal from my father's dresser.

The saints turn their faces into the walls, away from the sight
of so many waxen hopes.

Cracked Plymouth vinyl burning the backs of our thighs as we
counted saguaros for thirty miles.

The day you found your baby tooth in my wallet and called
me hopeless.

I hand you a candle and you put it between the turned-out feet
of St. Francis.

The pomegranates we eat compulsively, the way the fruit
numbs our mouths.

A poem I wrote for you that you hated because I called you slick-backed and straw-veined.

Summer. A cracked mission rising from the desert.
The quality of light.

The mornings you call before breakfast to read me headlines.

We open the door to leave, and the arches of the ceiling falter at the sudden brightness.

The smell of you: turpentine, smoke, apricot.

You gasp at the first rush of heat. The fish in the courtyard mimics you.

I say, "What did you wish?"

The stone cat's whiskers tremble above us.

The two years we lived together and got our periods every month on the same day.

You open your hand to show me the miniature heart and say, "Nothing."

The mission pales behind you. Its faint histories of rain grow wider.

You say, "I didn't trust that shriveled little man." You say, "Take it."

The desert's stiff exhalations.

The way your fingers fumble as you remove the silver chain
I gave you for your last birthday and slide the charm onto it.
The way the clasp pinches my skin as you fasten it.

Places to find *milagros*: saints' dresses, gift stores, rearview
mirrors, buried in backyards.

The tin heart whispers as it shifts over my collarbone.
I say, "This is a mistake."

You squint as if you don't hear me.

Step closer to me so your face won't be in shadow.

You say, "Shh, I am remembering something."

All the Day's Sad Stories

A Novella

Some Kind of Omen

This is the year of beautiful trees. Cold nights, bright days, roadsides aflame. The wind blows, and maple leaves splatter the sidewalk. Mercy and Jake stand in the front yard raking. She has never had a false alarm; the blood comes as regularly as ever. Hopes are kept banked. The waiting extends only two weeks. It makes Mercy feel as if she is in some kind of dream in which they aren't really trying at all. Or as if the world in which she is living and breathing and menstruating is divorced completely from the landscape of her mind, which is cluttered with tired images of seeds and buds and petals unfolding, fruit ripening. The next morning, Mercy sees the first ginkgo leaf break from the tree and hurries outside. Dying, old, perseverant locusts rasp on the trunk; the leaves come down like wings slicing against her face. In less than twenty minutes it is over; the branches are clean, and a circle of gold spreads around her.

Roadside Attractions

One day, surprised by her reflection in a store window, Mercy realizes she is aging. The meat of her face is beginning to sag and pool. Her neck has a crepe-paper cast. She is thirty-seven, and it is ridiculous to be noticing such things. Bone loss, birth defects, mammogram. These are the words that float up to her from the car radio. She loves museums. She'll stop for anything claiming to be one, even those in people's houses by the side of the road. In Yuma, she paid two dollars to see an old man's collection of forks. They were arranged in cardboard soda flats lined with felt. One fork had a picture of Truman on the handle. In Kansas, a sign for a museum of *Horrors and Oddities* led to the detached garage of a blue ranch house. Metal shop shelves were stacked with boxes. A man sitting in a nylon and aluminum lawn chair inside the garage asked what kinds of oddities she was looking for. "Teeth, skulls, fetuses?" he said. She said she wasn't really into body parts. "Sweetheart, it's all body parts," he said. He asked what she did for a living. Then he took a box from the shelf next to him. It was close at hand, probably the first thing he showed everyone. It was a lampshade with no lamp, translucent and browning. "Human skin," he said. "Circa Nazi." That museum was free.

Mercy is flipping the deck of yoga cards, looking for her next pose. Jake is in the bedroom playing Internet poker. This is what he does when he is not at his flyspecked office in the history department or at yet another training camp on passive resistance. Ticking signals the dealing of hands. It sounds like a roulette wheel or a leaf caught in the spokes of a bike. *Vrikshasana*, tree pose; Mercy wobbles. She stares at her *driste*, her focal point, which is the thermostat on the wall. It is one of those old ones, brassy and pregnant with numbers. When the heat clicks on, a blue spark shoots out. Jake's Internet poker name is *lowluck99*; he says it is best to pretend you are a bad player to trick all the other players who are also pretending. When someone enters the table with a name like *acesonly* or *TeddyKGB*, you know he's a chump. *Ardha Chandrasana*, half moon, "I surrender into the flow of life." Outside, children are shrieking. Mercy remembers a game she played as a child called "statues" in which the goal was to stay frozen mid-motion as long as possible. This now strikes her as a game made up by adults. Jake types in the bedroom. The players talk to each other via a little column that runs alongside the graphic of the poker table. They use abbreviations to comment on hands: *TY* for thank you, *FY* for fuck you, *TYFY* for thank you and fuck you, *NH* for nice hand. Eight months they have been trying now; they have different opinions on what magic might work. Mercy breathes out and sings *Om*, "I am a part of Life's joyful sound," four parts: ah / oh / mmm / silence.

Experts Recommend the Missionary Position

When they make love, Jake lights incense from Tibet. Mercy wears her kimono with the embroidered rabbit. To know it is the proper time, she uses a digital thermometer made in Germany. She places a dense Swedish foam pillow under her hips. The sheets are antique linen bought in Paris; they are worn thin from years of loving and washing on the part of a French farmer and his wife. Waiting on the bedside table is a pot of tea, the leaves harvested in Africa, packaged in cheap pastel paper boxes labeled with the names of ailments, and located in the grocery store's natural foods section. The rug is from Iran, the bookshelf from West Virginia. The condoms Jake used were made in Canada and have maroon wrappers; now, they linger in his sock drawer like love letters. The white-noise machine has many components, some from Mexico, some from Taiwan. Next to the teapot is a small fat rock that they found on a beach in Texas. Afterward, Mercy lies still and listens to the Williams-Sonoma egg timer tick off the minutes with metallic pings; this is the sound of hope. Under the bed: months of dust. It is bad luck to sweep there when trying to call a child home. It is bad luck to throw anything out.

Why Mercy Makes Hats

The mystery of them—the old-time tilt and shadow. Black netting casting constellations over noses and cheeks. The fedora's come-hither modesty, the pillbox's nod to convention. Her grandfather owned a millinery shop in Des Moines sixty years ago. He had a blond-ringletted girl front for him, and he ordered hats and gloves from New York and San Francisco. They came in paperboard boxes cushioned in pink-tinted newsprint, smelling chemical, festooned with small hard fruits that popped white foam if pressed too hard. During the war, when the hats were all plain straw and skimpy felt, he ran a black market in silk stockings, which he kept under the counter in industrial-sized rat poison tins. His customers would kiss him thanks—waxy, crimson prints that earned him eye-rolls and gelid roast beef at home. The store folded in the late sixties, and he folded soon after, when Mercy was just a child, hardly old enough to remember his stories, the boater he constructed of blue typing paper, the lethal dust that sifted from a stretch of silk.

They Say Love the Skin

The sidewalk outside the coffee shop is littered with handbills promoting garage bands and diet supplements. Sometimes Jake is so quiet, especially in the car, that Mercy wants to run into something just to get a reaction. Her friend Morris says he spent his Saturday night hunting down cough syrup for his son. He went to three drugstores with the child strapped in his car seat, wheezing angrily. "The doctor said only brands without dextromethorphan." Mercy brushes a beetle off her napkin. Its wings open, glossy and iridescent, as it drifts to the table leg. "And then he won't touch anything grape- or cherry-flavored. Three years old and he already knows his own mind." Morris tells how he left the child in the car, shuddering with phlegm and weariness, while he went into each store. He says people were giving him dirty looks, but what do they know about a sick child. At the last drugstore, the one where he finally found the right medicine, bubble-gum-flavored, a man in an Army jacket stopped him on his way in. He asked Morris to buy him Evan Williams and knew exactly how much it cost. He had it in coins. "He said they didn't want him coming in there anymore." Mercy sees the way her life is going to go: coffee with friends, silent car rides, plucking stray hairs from her face, shopping trips to large cities. Morris hits the table with the flat of his hand. "I bought for him, of course. I bought for him."

September Nights, the Sky Blushes

Mercy reads the web forums moderated by female nurses and fertility experts with porn star names: Tiffany Titus, R.N., Ginger Mellon Bonaparte C.N.M. They are having a spate of what used to be called Indian summer. Even with the windows open and fans roaring, the house is steamy. Weeds are rotting in the drainage ditches, and by mid-afternoon, there is a haze in the air, stagnant clouds sifting down. The liveliest thread on the websites is about "motility issues." "Have hubby take a cold shower thirty minutes before sex." "Have hubby drink a cup of coffee—give the spermies a boost!" Baby talk for the childless. Mercy and Jake take turns watering the grass, clusters of gnats sticking to their knees. They have become superstitious about pleasure. She has spent hundreds of dollars on lingerie in the last eight months; the snap of elastic makes her think of her credit card. The weatherman is perpetually saying that this is the hottest year on record. At night, in the dark bedroom, sweat rises at the smallest touch. Mercy hangs her satin corsets and filmy underwear on the clothesline in the corner of the backyard, where they bulge and twist with the barometric pressure, as if trying to seduce the air.

Mercy and Jake Fight in the Kitchen

He leans against the sink. She sits on the lip of the cabinet that holds the good china. Neither one of them ever bothers to polish the silver. He has just come back from a run and is shirtless, skin swelling from heat and salt. His nipples are perfectly aligned, only slightly darker than his skin, wrinkled like eyelids squeezed shut. The dog eats its food without looking up. These are long, happy fights. Jake says, "Her hair is clearly red; how can you not see that?" Mercy says, "The plot wasn't even consistent." They switch positions mid-argument. Mercy chops carrots; Jake scoops out the rice. He levels the grains in the metal measure with his fingertips. They listen to Billie Holiday or the evening news as they cook. A little sadness makes the water boil faster. Another forest fire, a mudslide, an earthquake. A suicide bomber in a hotel pool. An air strike on a wedding party. When the flour tips off the counter onto the linoleum, their footprints materialize like magic, ghost steps, a diagram for dancing.

A Season of Darkened Parlors

This is the year of nine hurricanes. Mercy loves the whole system of it, the alternating names that transform the storms into petulant cousins or strange great-aunts and -uncles, the visitors who will not leave. She would not be so sanguine if she didn't live halfway across the country where the storms peter out in flurries of rain and hail. As a teenager, Mercy read only tales of true love and stigmata stories. She Googles "hurricane names," finds the FEMA-for-kids website, and is happy to live in a country that packages disaster for children. In dreams, faceless lovers and mysterious wounds still appear—fantasies of being chosen. She learns that only women's names were used for hurricanes until 1979. She learns that the list for Atlantic hurricanes may include French, Spanish, and English names. There is no explanation of which languages may be drawn upon for Pacific hurricanes. The romances she has given up, but she can't resist a good stigmata. On the satellite photo, a hurricane is an ephemeral thing, a veil of spinning mist. Sergio, Olaf, and Georgette. Flossie, Seymour, and Wallis. Visions of silent-film stars and bingo nights. Recently departed distant relatives summoned as if in séance, safe in a circle of clasped hands.

Mercy Employs Three Women
with the Names of Saints

Catherine B., Catherine P., and Bridget crimp and sew and harden hat forms all day in a rented storefront downtown next to the bank. They are thirty years older than Mercy and call her *honey pie* or *sweetpea* when they are angry. They wear gasmask-like filters when they work with fixatives or fire-retardant. Mercy tells them her troubles; the buzz of the sewing machine loosens her tongue. One day, the mayor stops by on his tour of local businesses, and the Catherines fuss over him and force him to eat a brownie. Bridget ignores him because of the zoning decision that allowed a Walgreens to be built at the corner of her neighborhood. From her office upstairs, Mercy hears Catherine B.'s seal laugh and smells acrid whiffs of sizing and scalded coffee. She provides them with health insurance and Christmas bonuses and a refrigerator stocked with Diet Coke. They give her advice-column stories of surprise babies and chocolate-flavored calcium chews. They are hopeful and resigned at the same time. They get calls on their cell phones from their grown-up, moved-out children and their retired husbands that involve phrases like *cream of mushroom soup*, and *the third time's the charm*, and *it was there yesterday*.

At the Grocery Store, Mercy Selects the Super-Sized Bag of Corn Chips

It is autumn and late at night and the moon is shriveling like a mum. Mercy buys olives, soda water, bright red pistachios. She has cravings; sometimes she licks salt off her index finger if there is nothing else in the house. The store is air-conditioned and fluorescent. There is a frost warning for tonight. Mercy and Jake wrapped their shrubs with burlap, and now it looks like a row of decapitated heads rings their house. The sliding doors at the front of the store whisper. Mercy has a hard time triggering automatic things—doors, faucets, towel dispensers. She spends a good portion of her time in public waving her hands at electronic eyes. In the fish section, the banks of ice are barren. The salad bar is lidded and dark. An old woman in a motorized cart is parked in the produce area. "There is no cilantro," she says plaintively. Mercy weighs limes in her palm. "There is no cilantro," the woman says again, this time as if in warning. Mercy brushes her fingertips across the paper skins of garlic, lifts a cantaloupe to sniff. Don McLean serenades the wide aisles. Somewhere, loaves of bread are rising.

The Catherines Sew Grandchildren's Costumes on Their Breaks

"Please not the fake fur," Mercy says. "We just had those machines oiled." Felt pumpkins, candy corn onesies, Red Riding Hood with ruffled panties —things to be gobbled. This is how the Catherines talk about the babies, as delicacies. "I just want to eat him up," they say. And, "Her hand is so perfect, I could bite it off." Hungry, aggressive grandmother love. Mercy knows the feeling, the ache in the jaw at the sight of a plump baby, the urge to chew and chew until that sweet thing is a part of her. When she was a teenager, they set up an X-ray at the mall on Halloween; kids in plastic skeleton outfits peered into the monitor at their ghost candy, waited for a needle or razor blade to fluoresce. Jake buys the most lumpish pumpkins he can find, the underrepresented pumpkins. Halloween night, they have few visitors. Their house is old and dark with a tipping porch, set back from the street. Morris comes with his son, who is dressed as a caterpillar or a leech. Mercy and Jake give him too much candy and go back to the doorway with their Tupperware bowl of packaged offerings, hoping their friendly silhouettes will draw the children. It's a pastoral scene: the scent of cider doughnuts and burning leaves, hollowed squash blackened by leftover citronella tealights, recorded moans blowing across the yard on wisps of nylon spiderweb. Miniature gods and demons drift down the street, demanding their empty sacks be filled.

Mercy and Morris Visit the Newly Painted Water Tower

It used to be striped rusty red and white, tea-stained and molting over the town. The pale blue paint makes the tower fade into the sky, and the town's name, stenciled in large black script, seems to float unmoored overhead. Morris's car is filled with burger wrappers and cases of generic diet cola. Mercy nudges a sock under the floor mat. Morris has been divorced a year; his beard is unkempt and he clutches her shoulder whenever he makes a joke. The scaffolding is still up on the north side of the tower. "Let's climb," Morris says. The layers of paint are lumpy on the cold rungs and her sandals slip before catching. Once they reach the top, the town is spilled before them, so quiet that she hears the courthouse clock hiccup before it chimes the half hour. She hiccups too, suddenly absurdly aware of time's passing. Morris puts his hand on her shoulder. "It's nothing," she says. They eat lunch in the car. Morris takes a carton of cut-up vegetables and a shaker of salt substitute out of a paper sack. Mercy has a bagel and a child-sized yogurt for which she has forgotten a spoon. He crunches away at half of a red pepper, and she thinks how bitter-sweet it is, the belief in self-improvement.

The First Real Snow of the Season
Comes on Thanksgiving

The streets disappear, and Jake and Mercy hole up in the house watching the sci-fi channel. That evening, they unearth the snowshoes from the garage and head toward dinner at Jake's department chair's house. They take the shortcut over the golf course, leaning into each other as they slip down hills, and come out on the main street almost directly across from Mercy's shop. The electricity has held, and her hats glow in the window display like alien spacecraft, quivering in the draft. Other people are out on their snowshoes as well, whole families with babies bundled into carriers and dogs bobbing in the drifts. There is a carnival atmosphere, the scent of woodsmoke and roasting bird, the carrion yells of the children flinging snowballs. Jake takes her hand; the warmth radiates as if they are holding the heart of a small animal between them. When they get to the house, they unpack Ziplocs of nutmeg-scented mashed sweet potatoes from Jake's bag, their contribution, along with a bouquet of icicles pilfered from the bus shelter's overhang, sharp as knives, already melting.

Where Mercy Goes on Her Lunch Break
When She Feels the Need to Escape

In the medical park next door there is a Japanese garden in the atrium. Koi swim in a black plastic pond surrounded by philodendrons. She imagines herself on Mount Koya, the smell of cedar, the saffroned monks. Sick children have stolen the rocks from the Zen garden; people have put out their cigarettes in it. The plants are dusty and neglected, and the miniature trees have outgrown their shapes. In the corner is a lovely green-tiled fountain, topped by a perplexed Buddha. Mercy meditates to its plashing and the ding of the elevator. People file in coughing and file out rustling prescriptions and sample packets. Her favorite fish is the white one with pink blotches that flails out of the water periodically to ram the other fish as if angry with the world. She loves this forgotten garden, the surly fish, the elevator behind her grinding its vertical path, a string of chakras spinning, the way it flings its doors open each time it returns, even if nobody waits.

On Clear Nights, Glow Is Visible

This is the year of volcano watches. The temperature below the surface surpasses the scientists' instruments. Jake comes home on the last day of the semester and announces he has quit his job in order to play Internet poker. Mercy says, "On the computer?" Jake looks at her as if she is an idiot. He says, "Last week, I made a $700 profit." Mercy realizes her hatmaking business is now their primary support. It seems a flimsy thing on which to base a household. The homes in the path of the lava flow have been evacuated. On the news, an orderly procession of minivans and small SUVs winds down the highway into the valley. A hard perimeter has been established, so the cameras are using hyper-zoom, which causes almost invisible pixilation. Jake explains the system of Internet poker tournaments and the philosophy of gambling as a career. He outlines cutoff points and timetables and gives her a chart of the odds. She learns if you are dealt a suited king and queen you have a 7 percent chance of winning the hand. Non-suited: 6 percent. Vulcanologists have set up a live video web-cam near the dome to record activity and entertain the masses. Whenever a blast of ash is released, the website goes down due to too much traffic. The movement of the ash one hundred feet straight into the air is a matter of hearsay and snapshots.

Jake's Mother Comes for Christmas, Eight Days Early

She strokes her lipstick-pink, leather-covered hip and says, "Still fits." She says to Mercy, "You are like the niece I never had." She puts metallic bows in the dog's hair. Brenda owns a Quick Stop in Indianapolis and can only visit for a few days at a time and never on an actual holiday. She punches Jake hard in the chest when he tells her about quitting his job and says, "All those student loans." Mercy thaws the turkey in the sink. They mouth Christmas carols while driving around counting blow-up Santas. Brenda says, "I like those icicle lights—looks like the house is making an effort." She works all day to paint "Joy to the World" in frosted letters on the front windows. At night, Mercy and Jake whisper in the guest room so his mother can have the firm mattress. Brenda finds the ovulation calendar with its Xs and Os in the bathroom drawer and cries. She says, "Why didn't you tell me you were trying?" She says, "All my life has been a disappointment." On the day of the premature dinner, five inches of snow fall. A potato in the bag in the pantry has gone rotten and bled white sap over everything. Whenever Mercy goes out to the porch where Brenda stands in the cold, smoking, to ask for her opinion or help, Brenda says, "You do it. I'm sure you know best."

In Mexico, They Are Happy

On Christmas Day, the sand burns the soles of their feet as they take turns walking up the beach to the fancy hotel for beers for Jake and virgin daiquiris for Mercy. They are staying in a hut thatched with ancient palm fronds where the ripped mosquito netting has turned sulfurous yellow. At night, large cockroaches bounce off them and roll like earrings under the bed. They kiss over whole fried snappers and raw squid while a man in the street exhorts them to buy from his box of sunglasses. "No, *gracias*, no," Jake says. He turns up his palms when he bargains with a woman for a wooden wind chime carved with scowling missionaries and says, "That's all there is." In the water, rust-colored jellyfish drift around them. A boy gathers newspapers and trash from the beach to make into handbags. The sun is slow to sink and the ocean stays tepid all night. They fall asleep to the clatter of dead priests.

One Month after Jake Quits His Job

They go to the Indian casino down the highway. Mercy means it as a gesture of solidarity. She counts mileposts and wreaths of roadside casualties. A shuttle painted turquoise takes them from the parking garage to the lobby. They eat overpriced lo mein and hot and sour soup in a restaurant called The Lucky Lotus. Mercy's fortune cookie says *Treasure what you have*. Jake's cookie is missing its slip. "Empty fortune," he says and crushes the cookie onto the bill tray. He kisses her hand as they walk past the craps table. He is a like a child waking from a nap. The ringing of the slot machines sounds like a thousand barcodes being scanned. Jake pulls a baseball cap out of his coat pocket and a pair of sunglasses. "Are we in disguise?" Mercy asks. Jake pinches her neck to hush her and veers toward the poker tables. Mercy puts two dollars worth of nickels into a game modeled on *The Addams Family* before buying a magazine and licorice whips at the gift store. In the faux courtyard, she perches on the edge of a fountain spewing dyed water and watches truck drivers and widows line up for free backscratchers in the shape of tomahawks.

On the Way Home

"You need new wiper blades," Mercy says. Jake doesn't say anything. He has lost twenty dollars at the casino. She has lost six
hours of her life and two rolls of nickels. Sleet smears the windshield, obscuring the dark road. When they meet another car,
the water glows on the glass. The wipers click along at the lowest
setting. "You might need to turn those up." Mercy feels mean
and just wants to be in bed. Fog snakes off the pavement. Jake
closes his eyes, and she flicks him on the shoulder. He opens his
eyes but doesn't look at her. He closes his eyes again. This is a
game they used to play when they were dating. She would reach
over and steer. Now, she clicks the lighter into its socket and
imagines the faint hiss of it heating. The patches of clear glass
are growing briefer. They hit the dog going around a curve. Its
body flies up onto the hood and into the windshield in front of
Mercy's face. A maze of cracks blossoms. She hears it hit the roof,
and then they are slowing, pulling to the side of the road. It is
Jake who gets out of the car and walks back. She sees him in the
side mirror, crouched on the shoulder, a pinpoint of blue from his
keychain LED. A car swerves around the curve and he is caught in
the glare, head ducked, almost unrecognizable.

The Dog's Tags and Rabies Vaccination Number Are Small Tin Hearts

Jake holds the dog wrapped in his parka; Mercy rings the door-bell. It is four o'clock in the morning and there are two lights on. From their right comes the rattle of a garage door opening. The dog's owner is a large man with creases like cuts in the flesh of his neck. The garage is cluttered with half-folded newspapers. "For my son's route," the man explains, before they can say any-thing. He has been stuffing the papers into plastic sacks to pro-tect them from the weather. Jake holds the dog out to him and tells him the story, too quickly. The man doesn't take the dog but wraps one of the bags around his knuckles saying, "Wait, slow down." Jake thrusts the dog at him, and the man backs into a column of papers. As Mercy restacks them, the man starts crying. "It's too much," he says, as though they have brought him an expensive gift. Jake lays the blue nylon bundle on the only empty chair; one sleeve slithers loose and makes them all start. The smell of wood pulp and wet ink fills the garage. There is nothing to do now but leave. In the car, backing down the long driveway, Mercy says, "You just bought that jacket," as she searches between the seats for a napkin, afraid to look at Jake, her fingertips silky with plane crashes and robberies, drug busts and congressional panels, all the day's sad stories.

In February, Mercy Imagines Summer

They have a terrific fight over mail-order seedlings. Mercy fingers the manila catalog as if it is a letter from her long-dead grandmother, thinking of fat peppers and corn and cucumbers, all in a row. "Don't we have enough problems?" Jake yells. He invokes weeding and borers and hungry deer. He is furious at the asking price for flats of early-producing tomatoes. They rapidly move on to his mother, the times Mercy forgot to mail the gas bill, the number of instances they've washed each other's laundry or had to repark the other's car. Indifferent winter binds the house. To annoy her, Jake goes ice-climbing in a snowstorm. What he doesn't know is how her relief at his coming home safely will be mixed with regret that no terrible thing happened to punish him. To escape her own pettiness, she goes snowshoeing in the same storm, taking the dog with her for company. The ice packs into the dog's paws until trickles of blood dot its footprints, and she pretends not to notice. In the snow, she could be anyone, a different person entirely. *Shush*, *shush* go the snowshoes until she is lost in the woods, the storm blown up into a near blizzard, and she finds a felled tree to sit down on, tucks the shivering dog behind her knees, waits for it to pass.

After the Storm

Thighs pink and prickled with the change from blowing snow to gusting central heat, Mercy sips cocoa in her rabbit-embroidered robe. Jake drops tiny marshmallows one by one into her mug. When they kiss, everything gets warmer. There is a slightly moldy leftover loveseat in the kitchen, too big to fit through the back door, and they end up there, sweaty, laughing, and underneath a sort of relief, an unexpected thaw. In the corner, the dog snuffles for crumbs. Outside, everything is frozen, muffled, the beautiful blue of midwinter. Inside, their cramped lovemaking beats like a pulse, the stutter of blood under skin. Mercy feels it when she touches him, the hundreds of other times they've done this. Suddenly, in the midst of the sweating and panting and giggling, the small jokes and sighs and misplaced elbows, she knows, feels the child locking into place inside her, glowing, a minute combustion spreading light. The snow continues to fall, completing its slow refiguring, the swells and drifts that make the world strange.

Mercy and Jake Go to a Dinner Party

The host tells them about his research on the mating rituals of fireflies. The male and female flash precisely timed patterns as courtship. Under the table their legs bump, Morse-code via kneecaps. After dinner, the hostess opens the fireplace flue and a dead bird drops out. Jake cradles it in paper towels and takes it to the outside trash. Returning, he trips and puts his hand through the door-side window. Blood drips across new carpet, and Jake catches it in the cup of his hand. A bird, a cut, the night is over before a match is struck. Days later, Mercy kisses the rind of scab that bisects his palm. She blows his hair out of his eyes. Frost limes the windows. Ice slides down the roof. Tree branches crack where they touch.

Three Weeks Late,
Because Three Is a Lucky Number

She watches two blue lines snake up in the plastic window, charmed by her urine. Seven weeks late, because seven is a magic number, the blood seeps out of her and stains the mattress. She dreams of jars filled with ruby red marmalade. She dreams lids sterilizing, flat brass disks, so pleasing with their crimson rubber rings. She dreams her grandmother peeling oranges in one long strip, a sun shedding its skin. The next morning she reads about a man who saw Jesus in a fishstick just as he was about to feed it to his dog, auctioned it on EBay, and made $200,000. Her high-school friend's father told her naked women were everywhere, and then he pointed one out on the macaroni and cheese box and in the Bailey's ad and on the kitchen windowpane. The cinnamon toast burned as he ran his hand under her blouse, and her friend sang from the basement, *"Where have you gone?"*

Jake Remarks that Saffron Costs More per Ounce than Gold

This is the year of beheadings, garage sales, rising gas prices. At the Italian market, Mercy says, "How are we going to afford a child if we can't afford olive oil?" The old men owners tsk over the fresh pasta cooler. To mollify them, she buys two pounds of whole wheat linguine, the least popular noodle. The old men take turns easing the nests of pasta into a recycled bread bag. They tell her not to refrigerate it, to leave it in the dark pantry. "Let it rest," they repeat. Mercy and Jake argue over the cost of haircuts, video memberships, bottles of wine for friends' parties, plain black T-shirts, camping equipment, and photo developing. He keeps adjusting the setting on the hot water heater so the shower runs cold just as she starts shaving her left leg. She never says the phrase, "If you hadn't quit your job," but she holds it there in the space between them, like any one of the objects that cause them such unhappiness.

One Morning, while Scrubbing the Rust from Her Gardening Tools in Preparation for Spring

Mercy finds a white X chalked next to the hose holder. She crouches to touch it and the lines smear into the slate-colored siding. It took months to decide on the color, and then they painted the house themselves, in dribs and drabs over two weeks last summer. Sometimes still, pulling into the driveway at dusk, one of them will say, "Is it too dark?" Now, wrapping the hose around the metal bracket, she wonders how the X got there. A survey crew of some sort recording a gas line or a water main? Perhaps a child playing a skewed game of tic-tac-toe? The yard is heavy with melted snow; crusts of ice crackle in the shade. Mercy thinks of Xs painted onto trees in the forest, marking them for removal. She thinks of a tangle of pipes stretching like roots through the neighborhood. She imagines her neighbors all showering at once, chorus of waters underfoot.

Mercy Picks Up Her Niece from Music Lessons

The little yellow house is dark, always dark. Oboes and clarinets hang in rows on the living room wall, moaning in the draft. Her niece puts two sticks of gum in her mouth the minute they get in the car. She is fifteen and collects antique birdwatching guides. They pick up her friend and head downtown. The girls huddle in the back seat whispering about sloe gin fizzes. "I could only drink a sip," her niece says. Streetlights trill in the increasing rain. "He has a bad-ass tattoo of Andy Warhol," the friend says. The girls pull on their work clothes in the backseat. The tax-prep franchise hires them to stand on the street corner and wave at cars. Her niece is the Statue of Liberty with a turquoise nylon poncho and a rubber torch. The friend is Uncle Sam with a tall striped hat and a moustache that is already peeling. They tumble out of the car singing thank yous and start dancing in what Mercy assumes is a patriotic manner under the Don't Walk sign. Uncle Sam snaps her suspenders at two paramedics stalled at the red light. The Statue of Liberty grins despite the green run-off from her foam spikes that patinas her face. Under the front seat, the clarinet rattles in its plastic case, forgotten again.

Mercy and Morris Eat Donuts by the River

This is the year of recalled vaccines and hoarding and old people fainting in line. He tells her he is learning to speak French to impress women. "Potential dates," Mercy says. Morris nods and says, "From a set of tapes for the car—French for Commuters." The river is fat from the spring melt, and sticks and strange objects hurtle by the boulder where they are perched. "*Au voleur*," Morris says, "Stop thief." A sour cream container rushes past them. "*Je suis de passage*, I'm just passing through, *Je suis célibataire*, I'm single, *Il pleut*, it's raining." "Impressive," says Mercy. By midwinter, the rationing and panicked purchases from Canada resulted in doctors' refrigerators filled with rapidly expiring vials. Morris takes Mercy's hand and announces, "*Avec des glaçons*, on the rocks." "Different rocks," she says. "*Je ne peux pas bouger la jambe*, I can't move my leg, *Il manque un couteau*, there is a knife missing." Caught in an eddy are a pink dishwashing glove and a bunch of dead leaves. "*Je crois que je sui perdu*, I think I'm lost." Mercy kisses Morris on the mouth, grabbing the back of his head so hard that he grunts. Their teeth touch and she tastes the rough sugar from the donuts, grainy and brittle at the edges of their lips. Then she is facing the river again, panting, feeling a pain in her throat. Something that might be a dead animal floats by, a mass of hair and skin. Morris is grinning, and she says, "Stop it; it's not a good thing." She says, "This doesn't change anything." He says, "*Je comprends un peu*."

After Kissing Morris

Mercy runs the high school track until her hips feel like doll's joints. She is excessively polite to bank tellers and gas station attendants. She can't get the window display in her store right. The aqua gauze symbolizing the blue skies of April snags on her fingernails. Hats fall from their hooks. The dog barks uncontrollably late at night, and the neighbor sprays it with her hose. Mornings, she practices holding her breath until Jake wakes up. Fifty-eight seconds until she sees black. They bike in the ever-earlier dawn, wrapped in layers of spandex and polypropylene. Jake tells her to stop pushing the big gears and spin. The derailleurs clack like ice breaking. He says to relax, and she feels her knees loosen. He says everything naturally gravitates toward efficiency. She watches the thin strip of his back wheel and intuits the road ahead from its movement.

When the Bird Feeder Goes Missing, Mercy Blames the Squirrels

It has suddenly warmed into full spring, and her shoes clump with mud as she searches the shrubs beneath her kitchen window for the feeder. Later in the day, she finds it, propped against the door that leads to the crawlspace beneath their porch. When she carries it back around the house, bemused, she finds the X, chalked next to the kitchen window, small, up high, like a sleepy moth. The jolt that goes through her is the kind of fear one feels at an accidental cut. She is afraid to look directly at it. When she tells Jake about it and the first one, by the spigot, that she hadn't thought to mention, he is confused, as if these are figments of her imagination made solid. That night, they make a curry and spend a long time chopping side by side in the kitchen. The oil gets hot in the pan and the mustard seeds jump. The kitchen window grows dark as the world closes around them, the light space of the room, the smell of onions frying.

Awash

This is the year of overabundance. Storms saturate the desert into new blooms and the Great Salt Lake rises and butterflies that no one has seen in fifty years unfurl. And the stock market bulges slowly like a flooded river and the beef that Japan doesn't want rots on refrigerated shelves. Mercy's Aunt Geraldine dies, and she sorts her things, culling vintage laces and trims she can use for her hats. In her closet are thirty-two white broadcloth shirts and six pairs of unworn New Balance walking shoes. In the kitchen, two coffeepots still in their boxes. The garage is orderly, and the cedar chest holds stacks of tablecloths and embroidered pillowcases. These, Mercy holds to her cheek to test the thread count. An ancient Hershey's cocoa tin holds bone buttons and blackening snaps. The silk wedding dress tears on its hanger. Mercy's pile is growing. Then she finds the scrapbooks, the post-cards glued like specimens on the ridged paper. Geraldine had an African safari fund she never used or gave away even when the osteoporosis crippled her. Boxes of screws and nails labeled by size bow the workshop shelves. Mercy's fingers grow numb with the sorting. She and Jake need to have a spring cleaning of their own. Like the pill bugs fringing the baseboards, her hopes curl in on themselves. Next to the kitchen sink, Geraldine's ashes settle in their paper box. In California, botanists name new flowers after stepchildren and second cousins, grade-school teachers who smelled of cardamom and stale polyester.

Mercy Spends All Week Pinning, Sewing, and Gluing Flowers onto Hats

Redbook's "Summer Fashions on a Budget" featured one of her hats, and she is buried under requests for pale citron bowlers trimmed with white silk peonies. Her fingers are spotted with hot glue burns and punctures from the wire stems. On the weekend, she plants azaleas in the corners of the yard, blankets them with ammoniac mulch. They are already flowering, and she admires their lacy fans; Jake, cranky from a bout of lawn mowing, says the blooms look like cat vomit. They stand in the hollow of their yard, and he rubs her shoulders, nuzzles the sweat off her neck. She counts backward and says, "Tuesday." Early Monday morning, Jake comes in from getting the paper and says, "Something strange has happened." The azaleas are laid out in a row on the front yard, their roots spidery and drying. The holes in the flowerbeds glare at Mercy, and when she turns to go inside, she sees the X on the doorjamb, thickly chalked, a closed eye. "Children," Jake says, and she imagines them, curled in their tight houses, blinded like puppies by sleep. "Children," she repeats and heads to the garage for the trowel and her gardening gloves. The sun is just coming up, a low hum on the horizon.

Jake Falls off the Roof
into the Mulberry Tree and Is Unhurt

Things like this are always happening to him. Mercy carries a travel first aid kit and copies of their insurance cards in her purse. The tree is a white mulberry the first owners of the house brought back from China seventy-five years ago. Later in the summer, swollen lavender fruit will droop like pupas from the tree. Jake is still lying under it, new leaves in his hair, twigs for an aura, when she finds him. The original owners hoped for silkworms, not knowing they could no longer fly and thus existed only in captivity. "There is a huge spider web on the side of the house up there," he says. This is the kind of thing he notices while falling from great heights. Once they pull the ladder around, they discover it is not a spider web but another X, chalked fuzzily in the space directly beneath their bedroom window. Even though Jake washes it off, late that night, Mercy feels its shadow, imagines some large dust-intestined insect watching them sleep, jealous of their warmth, their white sheets, their filaments of breath.

Mercy Meets Morris's Ex-Wife, Lydia, for Lunch at the Mall

Her basal temperature tells her she is ovulating. She and Jake had sex twice in the last three days. The Chinese gender chart says their child, if conceived this month, would be a boy. She enters the mall through the lingerie section of a department store. Past the mesh bras and tap pants are the children's clothes, a joke, she wonders, natural progression? By habit, she resists looking at the baby clothes; any act of imagination feels like a jinx. Lydia is waiting by the Taco Bell, wearing one of Mercy's hats. She looks awful in it, and Mercy feels momentarily angry at the thought of all those unsuitable women buying her hats, paying for her lunch and her shoes and her gynecological exams. They sit by the carousel with their trays of mall-Asian food—eggroll, lo mein, plastic pillow of sweet and sour. "You've been keeping secrets," Lydia says. "Morris told me all about it." Children drag by on the creaky carousel, and Mercy feels a pang deep in her gut, an egg releasing, fear, a kiss, an X on the doorjamb, a hatch mark on the calendar. "Your hat was in *Redbook*," Lydia says, holding her hand to the crown of her hat as if the carousel is kicking up a wind. "I dug this out of my closet—it was in the Salvation Army pile," she laughs. "One more month and it would have been gone." Mercy leans forward and tips Lydia's hat back on her head, rests her hand on the curve of her neck. She says, "I guess I got lucky."

They Start Finding Xs Every Other Day or So

On the paving stone closest to the storage shed, the red flag of the mailbox, every fence post in the backyard, appearing one by one like light bulbs flicking on. On the spare wheel of Jake's Jeep, the clapper of the bamboo wind chimes. The potting soil is dumped in a mound in the backyard, the bag knotted around the front doorknob. Their garbage cans are knocked down, dented; they find their newspaper burnt on the walk. "It's some kind of campaign," Jake says, and they stay up late, peering from their dark living room. In the bedroom, Mercy pulls a chair next to the window and watches the yard swell and diminish in the moonlight. They set amateurish traps, a video camera whose tape runs out, a string of bells on the garden gate, a drugstore motion detector alarm on the driveway. They don't call the police or quiz their neighbors. Without discussion, they both know there is a message here they must unravel. Jake talks about digging a pit and covering it with grass clippings. Mercy starts constructing her own semaphore; she leaves milk in an old tin pie plate for the neighborhood cats, paints their door Greek-isle blue, ostentatiously recycles. She ties paper lanterns onto the beams of the porch and washes the sidewalk in front of the house. She is broadcasting good intentions. The bells in the garden ring without provocation, on windless days, and Jake says, "Listen, the ghosts are at it again."

Mercy and Morris Meet
at the Cineplex Fifteen Miles Away

The Chinese film they are seeing is folded away in the smallest theater, and the only other people watching are two elderly women who whisper through the credits. Morris puts his hand over hers without looking at her. Mercy holds her breath as the colors stain the screen. A chartreuse dress, gold lanterns, indigo streets burnished by lamplight. The subtitles flash too brightly and create a sensation of flickering vertigo. Mercy turns to Morris, finds his mouth, sinks into a kind of oblivion, the long kisses she remembers from high school, the kind that went on until it wasn't about desire anymore, was simply the pursuit of texture, dark fleshy spaces that stretched until everything felt like an extension of one's own body. She relaxes into this moment, despite Morris's inept rubbing at her shoulders, the giant paper cup of soda with its straw squeaking between them, the chirps and gongs of the fight scene. When she pulls away, her mouth is tacky with saliva and Morris looks blissfully at her, *like a dog,* she thinks and is startled by her bitterness, the extent of her betrayal. She tries to pay attention to the movie, but the subtitles seem wrong for the action, and she doesn't know if it is because she has missed crucial information or if it is just shoddy translation. Her jeans are wet as if something inside her is weeping, flooding with the onscreen dialogue, a language she doesn't understand.

Suddenly, Everything Makes Mercy Paranoid

Someone is calling and hanging up. The chalk Xs continue to bloom on their property, and Jake refuses to get caller ID. Mercy hacks his hotmail account in search of chat room hussies and grad school crushes. She sniffs his underwear, finds only the musky almond scent of him, scans his shirt collars like a fifties housewife. At work, she goes over their finances while the Catherines mutter at their sewing machines. No plot is beyond imagination: offshore accounts, angry bookies, a looking-glass family in Tennessee. A gray Cadillac passes her twice while she is running; a woman in the coffee shop is wearing the same cardigan as she is. She imagines her china rearranged, a shadow in the bathroom mirror, every horror movie cliché burned into her brain during countless bad date drive-ins and basement sleepovers in high school. When she calls Morris to ask if he is stalking her, he says, "It was just a couple of kisses, pretend we were drunk." And then he laughs his horsey laugh, and she knows there is no way that Morris is creeping around her house at night. It is the season of thunderstorms that blow up without warning and a sky that darkens as if a filter has clicked into place. One evening, when the power has gone out and Mercy and Jake are sitting on the porch, lightning strikes the neighbor's fir tree. The air turns purple, their fillings hiss, and the light is so thick it hurts their sinuses. In that moment, she sees the figure in their yard, half hidden behind the elm. She runs toward the spot, leaving Jake shouting after her, knowing that nothing will be waiting there, just the smell of burning sap and loosed rain, the sound of water hitting skin.

The Spine Is a Delicate Evolution

"I'm mortified," Mercy tells her sister as they line up for yoga class. She is visiting her in New York amid meetings with department store buyers. Her sister is the one person she can tell about Morris because they aren't particularly close. They have a two-hour threshold for mutual tolerance, worked out after rooming together for a year of college and nearly killing each other over mildewed dishrags and borrowed belts. The yoga instructor greets them all with a half-bow and ushers them into the small, mirror-lined room. He is shirtless and his skin is ruddy-tan, stretched tight over his belly like a roasted pig. They start with cat tilts, and her sister whispers, "Is it serious?" "Of course not," Mercy hisses and feels the arch of her spine crimp. They face the wall for dancer pose, and Mercy says, "It's fucked up, right, making out with my best friend while my husband and I are trying to get pregnant?" She stumbles into her sister and they both yelp. The instructor squints at them and intones, "Get grounded." During boat pose, Mercy inhales the dust of the mat as her sister rocks placidly beside her saying, "You just needed a little attention." In corpse pose, she can feel every bone of her back touching the floor, and she imagines her body a crypt, each vertebra a walled-up secret. The instructor places his hands beside her ears to realign her head, and a small space opens at the base of her neck, radiates relief.

Trapped on the Subway
Due to a Fire on Another Track

The scratched Plexiglas gives the feel of an aquarium, one of those cheap globes at Kmart Mercy mooned over as a child, each studded with a plump goldfish that her mother refused to buy her because she said they wouldn't last a week. The car is on a section of track closed between two walls, and Mercy is late for an appointment with a woman who makes flowers out of old calligraphy workbooks, every petal an imperfect word. She scuffs her pumps against the accordion floor and reads the newspaper over the shoulder of the man next to her. Cancelled shuttle launches, grilled chicken recipes, bomb scares that turn out to be lunch sacks. At the last station, waiting for the train to arrive, she called Jake on her cell phone, had a frizzled conversation of last syllables and interruptions until she said "I miss you," and hung up, not sure what he heard. The walls were papered with Rodenticide warnings, forbidding people to touch or eat the bait without specifying what the bait was. A man slept on a folded blanket under the escalator while a woman next to him sat alert, scowling, as if daring anyone to disturb his delicate refuge. It broke Mercy's heart to see them, but then the train rattled in, blowing sweaty air in front of it, and she was pushing for a seat, not knowing yet about the fire burning ahead of them, not yet thinking of the orange fish and their conscribed pirouettes, their languorous acceptance of their fates.

Mercy Goes to Her Ob/Gyn for the Third Time This Year

Her doctor, who is a little Texan redhead, drawls, "It's time to start looking at other options." Pink plumes of reproductive propaganda flutter in the air conditioning. "Y'all have just about exhausted the natural route," she says and pats Mercy's paper-covered thigh, clicks her pen, draws a pamphlet on fertility treatments from her clipboard. She barely looks at Mercy's ovulation charts, four months cross-stitched with temperatures, mucus descriptions and do-it dates. In the park across the street, mothers yell at their children on the slides and Mercy tosses the doctor's pamphlets in the trash can atop ice cream ruins and yesterday's news. Although profoundly unreligious, she is superstitious, needle-phobic, lazy and in love with the romance of old-fashioned cock and womb, candlelit, sweaty, pungent reproduction. She figures this is a sign or more likely, a punishment for procrastination and that her best defense is graceful concession. She summons up glamorous trips, unencumbered old age, reading novels until noon, starts exchanging one fantasy for another. A chalked X greets her from her driveway, boxed like a hopscotch square, and she sneaks into the backyard to cry, knowing Jake is calculating the odds on the computer upstairs. The corner of the yard is overgrown and shady, and she crouches in the ferns. If she is quiet, she can almost hear someone else's heartbeat, someone else's breath, as if coming to her from a distance, from a future she hasn't yet imagined.

Jake Talks about Defoliants Over Dinner

Dioxin, demeton, cacodylic acid. Mercy takes this as a hopeful sign;
maybe he is missing his job, longing for a lectern, research trips,
access to microfiche. Miscarriage, mutation, birth defect. He rolls
the word, *teratology*, on his tongue with the black beans. Midway
through the meal, she goes to the kitchen for a bottle of wine and
two glasses. The look on his face is that of someone surprised by
disaster, the click of a land mine, the drone of a plane's engine.
"Pour it," she says. She is tired; in the crib of her pelvis, she feels
her ovaries wither. He fills each glass without spilling a drop, a
terrible competence. The bottle sounds heavier than it should
when he puts it down on the table. They sit without eating and
watch the resin spread like poison across the surface of the wine.

When Mercy Goes Outside to Pick Basil for Dinner

She finds a man crouching by her back door who fumbles chalk into his pocket, says, "I thought you weren't home. Your car ..." She says, "We're having the timing belt replaced," almost apologetically. When he turns his face toward her, she recognizes the man whose dog they hit, and she recoils as if the windshield is breaking in front of her again. Into the awkward pause she asks, "Would you like to join us for dinner?" When she goes upstairs to get Jake, he hisses, "There are limits to politeness." Back downstairs, at the kitchen table, the man sits with a sweating bottle of Corona untouched in front of him. Jake says, "Hi there buddy, long time no see, what have you been up to?" Mercy says, "It's not much, just pasta." Jake flings open the refrigerator and says, "Ham, we've got ham, and brie and look at these plums, gorgeous, big as fists." He is yanking food out and slamming it onto the table. "How about another beer?" He opens the rest of the six-pack of beers and puts them one by one in front of the man, pulls containers of olives and cherry tomatoes out of the refrigerator, piles pita bread atop takeout fried rice atop romaine. Carrots tumble over blocks of butter and eggs tremble at the edge of the table as the refrigerator rattles to life, leaks its cold air over them. The man doesn't touch a thing. Jake takes one of the beers and drinks it in noisy swallows, drops it onto the table where the bottle cracks into three pieces. Mercy says, "Please, Jake." The man reaches across the table for the shards, stacks them into a lopsided pyramid. Jake asks, "Have you ever seen plums that big?" softly, as if truly puzzled by their appearance.

What They Learn

All the man's knuckles are bruised brown, and Mercy wonders if he is diabetic. He works the night shift at the ammunition plant out by the interstate. He checks the plastic honeycombs filled with bullets as they slide down the line to the boxing station. If one slot is empty, his job is to find the proper caliber and fill it before the case passes out of reach. As the light fades, Jake rummages for candles. He finds two his nephew made him last year in a class project—wax-filled seashells that tip on the table as if rocked by invisible waves. During the day, the man refills candy machines at local restaurants. Mercy can imagine it perfectly, the click of the candy like bullets filling the glass jars, the sweet metallic residue the man washes from his hands each morning and evening. The beer is finally getting to Jake, and he says, "Why the Xs?" The dog whines at the door to be let in, and they all pretend not to hear it. The man fingers a bit of bread that has fallen next to his plate, rolls a ball and flattens it. "It's funny," he says, eyes trained on the row of crumbs he is aligning. "I used to yell at that idiot mutt ten times a day." Mercy touches his elbow, hesitantly. His arm goes still as if she is a wild animal he is afraid of startling. He says, "You guys are nice people, good people, I can tell." She clears the dishes as Jake leads him to the front door. Jake comes back with a plastic tub half-filled with Chiclets and says, "He wouldn't take no for an answer." Mercy remembers chicken-fried steak at a roadhouse called the Chuck Wagon near her grandmother's farm, the begged nickel, a handful of lacquered gum, the blissful ache of sugar seeping into teeth.

Mercy and Jake Go Backpacking

There is something she loves about it, beyond the trees and the lichen and the clear streams. It is the release of knowing the only things she has to think about are shelter and food, how to get from one point to the next. By the end of the third day, her shoulders and hipbones are too sore to be touched. Jake blows on them, singing songs he remembers from church camp. The tent is tiny, a nylon shroud they share. "What will we do now?" she asks. He sings, "All is well, safely rest." He says, "There is no limit to loveliness," and his breath floats over the raw places. Rocks push through the foam pads, and trees growing on the bones of those cut years ago inch toward the night sky. Everything struggles upward, as if the stars are apertures to brighter worlds. Mercy and Jake eat freeze-dried beef stroganoff with the map stretched between them. It belonged to his father, and its creases are white with use. Some things have changed: landslides, shifted rivers, dried-up waterholes, and new highways. They often are lost, often must rely on nostalgia to guide them.

Mercy Searches Out Small Graces

This is the year of missing children and confessed serial killers who go by acronyms like revamped fast-food restaurants. This is the year of media alerts, dead girls in cheerleading outfits, and alarmist digital-ticker headlines synchronized to symphonies in B minor. Mercy and Jake's neighbor believes the spirits of five children circle every woman's head, waiting to be called down into the bloody mess of her womb. She says her seventh child is one of theirs, a celestial adoption. In the driveway, over a borrowed pair of hedge clippers, she tells Mercy about the child's surprise asthma, the nine-hour emergency-room visit last week, the stockpile of hermetically sealed inhalers taking up the toothbrush drawer. She says all this while looking accusatorily at Mercy, or rather, at the space over Mercy's left shoulder. She says, "He is still our little angel though, a perfect angel." The ice cream truck squeals at the corner. Mercy opens and closes the clippers, *snip snip*, as if cutting holes in the neighborhood. All the missing children seem to pass through Florida. Mercy likes to imagine them there in the swamps, swaddled in mosquitoes and moss, feet happily muddy, wrestling the alligators, loving them for their bumps.

Like a Snake, a Cicada's Greatest Art Is Its Doubling

Late August. The things they planted have grown and been plucked or eaten or given away. No more Xs bloom on their siding. Jake builds a bonfire of vines and tree branches in the backyard. The charred ring that results is as solid as the moon. Mercy chews hard lozenges of gum and spits them into the garden or swallows them. *Seven years*, she thinks, but maybe that is bad luck and mirrors or growing a new skin. There is a lull in the evening news, and the anchors turn to politics and taxes. A new season of disasters is predicted, but no one can ever truly know what might happen. Earlier in the summer, they helped their entomologist friend tag cicadas with white dots. Each bug was a hard suitcase of longing and patience, difficult to hold—their hearts were so steady and droning. As a child, Mercy used to tie them onto strings and launch them into the air as if casting a bit of her own heart into orbit. Now, sitting on the porch with Jake, drinking day-old wine, she spots a paper-skin ghost of a cicada gripping her chair leg and is suddenly awash in happiness, recalling the way these somnolent insects sip tree sap and wait out the dark, the way they sing themselves from the ground.

Acknowledgments

Thanks to all the kind and patient editors who published stories from this collection in their super fabulous literary magazines and who were scrupulous and inspired in their edits. "By the Gleam of Her Teeth, She Will Light the Path Before Her" appeared in the *Collagist*. "Erratum: Insert 'R' in 'Transgressors'" appeared in *3rd Bed*. "Faith Is Three Parts Formaldehyde, One Part Ethyl Alcohol" appeared in the *minnesota review*. "For Dear Pearl, Who Drowned" appeared in *Water-Stone Review*. "In Your Endeavors, You May Feel My Ghostly Presence" appeared in *descant*. "There Is a Factory in Sierra Vista Where Jesus Is Resurrected Every Hour in Hot Plastic and the Stench of Chicken" appeared in *Quarterly West*. "This Is a Love Story, Too" appeared in *Fairy Tale Review*.

An extra special thanks to Joseph Reed and Amanda Raczkowski of the wonderful Caketrain Press who published "All the Day's Sad Stories" as a chapbook and made it more lovely than I ever could have imagined.

Much gratitude to The Corporation of Yaddo for a magical snowy February.

And many, many thanks to Drue Heinz, Renata Adler, and the University of Pittsburgh Press for putting their faith in this odd collection and making an actual book of it. I am especially grateful to Deborah Meade for her meticulous and intuitive edits.

Thank you to Trudy Lewis, friend, mentor, and writer extraordinaire, whose sense of humor and integrity have taught me how to make a writing life work. Thank you also to Jeff Williams, whose unshakeable support has been invaluable. And thanks to all of my friends, students, and colleagues at Hamilton College whose kindness and enthusiasm have made my teaching life a joy.

Love to all of my family, especially my parents, who never flinched when I talked about being a writer. And to Hoa, who always steps in to do what I cannot. And to Tycho, who came into my world and blew it apart in beautiful ways.

Book design and composition by Landesberg Design, Pittsburgh, Pa.,
typeset in Charter ITC and Whitney.

Printed by Thomson-Shore, Inc., on 60 lb. Natures Book Natural,
an FSC certified paper containing 30% post-consumer waste.